Daris Camp Adventures
A Transylvanian Saga

DACIAN DOLEAN

Daris Camp Adventures: A Transylvanian Saga

Copyright © 2022 Dacian Dolean

Cartoon Illustrations by Richard Duszczak –
TheCartoonStudio.com

ACKNOWLEDGEMENT

The work on this book was partially supported by two
research grants awarded to the author by the Ministry of
Research and Innovation from Romania, CNCS - UEFISCDI,
project number PN-III-P1-1.1-PD-2016-0164 and project
number PN-III-P4-PCE-2021-0072, and a grant awarded to
the author by EEA Grants 2014-2021, under Project EEA-RO-
NO-2018-0026, contract number 10/2019.

First edition, October 2022

ISBN: 979-8-3540-2541-1

Visit www.drdolean.com
Follow @DDolean

DEDICATION

To Lucas, Cristina, Ioan and Aurelia.

WARNING

This book contains a few passages that some readers might find

hilariously disgusting.

Read at your own risk!

PROLOGUE

"Danny, it's time to go!" Mr. Pop said to the closed door. "Get your bag and come downstairs."

"Dad, I'm not in my room." Danny's answer came immediately from behind the door. Mr. Pop opened the door and stepped inside. "You realize that your voice is coming from this room, right?"

"Well, it's not me. It's a recording," Danny's voice replied from under the bed.

"And how could a recording **predict** the answers to my questions?" Mr. Pop asked.

"Uh… I meant… uh…" Danny's voice started to sound a bit unsure.

"Danny. Your left foot is sticking out from under the bed. The hole in your sock is staring at me. It's **disturbing** and **unappealing**. Get out and let's go."

"Okay … Okay … I'm coming," mumbled the twelve-year-old as

he pushed himself out from under the bed. ***Disturbing****... How could a little hole in a sock **disturb** a big grown up like my dad?* thought Danny, dragging his feet on his way out of the room. *And since when are socks supposed to be **appealing**? I've never heard anyone saying, "Ooh, my socks are so **appealing**! All my friends tell me that if it weren't for my **appealing** socks, nobody would like me." I've never had my teacher tell me that I don't have to do homework as long as I wear **appealing** socks.*

"Look at this handsome young man," Mrs. Pop greeted her son as he came down the stairs. "Are you all packed and ready for a fabulous summer?"

"I am ready for a fabulous summer. I **predict** that if you would have let me spend the whole summer in my room with all my video games, my summer would have been fabulous. But that's not going to happen, thanks to you guys!"

"Oh, honey, I can imagine this trip might make you feel nervous. The first time in a foreign country can be a little bit **unsettling**," Mrs. Pop tried to comfort her son.

"Foreign country? You think that's what's bothering me?" cried Danny. "You could have picked a beach vacation in Greece. That would have been very **settling** for me. A cruise in Norway? Totally **settling**. A visit to Park Asterix in Paris? I can't think of anything more **settling** than that. But no! Why **settle** on a **settling** vacation? You had to choose THIS trip and send me to THIS camp!"

Mrs. Pop frowned. "How can you be so sure you won't like it?"

"Mom, I know I'll hate it!" yelled Danny. "The thought of this trip is completely **disturbing** and **unappealing** to me! More **unappealing** than the hole in my sock," said Danny as he stormed out of the house leaving Mrs. Pop puzzled.

In front of their house, the taxi driver was honking his horn. "Sir! Ma'am! I hate to remind you, but it's rush hour. If you want to get to the airport on time, we need to leave now!"

Rush hour? thought Danny. An evil **smirk** started to grow on his face. *Hmm...maybe there is hope. Maybe if I can delay my parents just a little bit longer....*

"Dad, I think I forgot my...."

"Don't even think about it!" said Mr. Pop, rushing everybody into the taxi. "Whatever you need, we can find it as soon as our plane lands."

"...passport," continued Danny. Mrs. Pop started to panic.

Mr. Pop calmly told the driver, "We are ready to leave." Then, turning to Danny, he pulled his son's passport from his jacket pocket. With a **smirk** he said, "Nice try. Anything else?"

"Fabulous", said Danny. He gave up. *I'm officially doomed*, he said to himself. *There is no turning back now. I know there is no rush hour in the world that could change my dad's mind. And THAT is a* **disturbing** *and an* **unsettling** *idea. He thought the hole in my sock was* **unappealing**? *Well, if you ask me,* **unappealing** *is when your parents plan to send you to a camp... in Transylvania!*

CHAPTER 1

Landing in Cluj-Napoca

The plane was **approaching** Cluj-Napoca, Romania. For the last hour, Danny had tried to keep his mind busy by watching a passenger who was sitting **adjacent** to him, on his left. The passenger was sleeping. His mouth was open, and now, he was drooling heavily on his own shirt. Danny had counted thirty-two big drops so far.

"Honey," Mrs. Pop said as she **approached** him, interrupting this enjoyable activity, "we are about to land. Do you feel any better now?" Danny's parents have been trying to **ease** his **anxiety** ever since they had boarded the plane. They told him that Cluj-Napoca was actually one of the largest cities in the Transylvania region of Romania and not at all a deserted and creepy place, as he had originally believed. Danny **disagreed** with them about the creepy part. All the stories he had ever heard about Transylvania involved blood and vampires.

"Mom, why would I feel better? Do you know that, as we speak, we are fast **approaching** - or even flying above - the spooky Hoia Forest? Do you think people call it the Bermuda Triangle of Romania for nothing? And this forest is **adjacent** to the city – not even in a **remote** location!"

Mrs. Pop said, "You're watching too much TV, baby. Remember, I grew up here. I played in Hoia Forest during my childhood. And I'm still here. You have no reason to **dislike** the city or feel **anxious**."

Danny **disagreed** again. "That's easy for you to say. All week you and Dad will be attending a conference in the city while I'll be stuck in the middle of nowhere ..."

"Only two hours away from us," Mrs. Pop interrupted again. "That is not very **remote** at all. I **predict** you will have a **fabulous** time at the camp. Remember, it will only last one week. It will be over before you know it."

Danny appreciated how his mom was trying to **ease** his **anxiety**, but he was still **unsettled**. He **agreed** that an adventure camp sounded **appealing**, and all the pictures he saw from the camp showed kids having a blast. However, he couldn't help thinking of all the stories he had heard about Transylvania. They were very **unsettling**. How could his parents be so sure that the vampires didn't exist? What if all the kids in the camp have to fight vampires every night? What if the kids in the camp ARE little vampires with little pointy teeth? What if ...?

A passenger who seemed in a rush interrupted his **anxious** train of thoughts. "Excuse me," she said, trying to get out of her seat and past the passenger sitting **adjacent** to her while everybody else patiently waited their turn. After bumping her neighbor on the head with her purse and stepping on another passenger's toes, she finally reached her destination. It was the luggage compartment above Danny's seat. *I didn't think they had **rush hour** on the planes*, thought Danny.

Then, as the lady stretched to reach her luggage, IT HAPPENED. Danny froze. He choked. His lungs refused to take in any air. He became as pale as a ghost. Then he fell flat in his seat and passed out.

CHAPTER 2

The Armpit Situation

"Honey, are you okay?" asked Mrs. Pop **anxiously**.

"I'm okay", said Danny opening his eyes. "What happened?" he asked.

"It looks like you **fainted** for a moment," said his mom. Mr. Pop **approached** Danny and said with a firm voice, "If this is another trick you are trying to pull to get out of going to camp...".

"No, Dad," interrupted Danny **abruptly**, **eager** to explain. "I can't make myself **faint**."

"So what happened?" asked Mr. Pop.

"Well, I did not come prepared to be caught in the middle of a biological warfare," started Danny. Mr. and Mrs. Pop looked **baffled**.

Danny explained, "You know, a combat situation when people use toxins as weapons of war... that is biological warfare." His parents were still confused.

Danny continued, "The lady that was so **eager** to get her luggage above my seat... well, when she stretched up her arms, the odor of her hairy armpits caught me off-guard. It was more than **disturbing**. It was **dreadful.** It hit me like a bomb! Just like a biological weapon. The smell got stuck inside my nostrils and I can't get it out. I think I'll have **nightmares** with hairy armpits for the rest of my life!"

"I totally agree with you," said Danny's dad very seriously. "You will have **nightmares** for the rest of your life."

"Really?" asked Danny.

"But there is a cure for that," continued his father as he took down the family's luggage and headed off the airplane.

"What is it?" asked Danny **eagerly**, following him and his mother onto the transfer bus.

"The only cure for your hairy armpit **nightmares** is going to Daris Camp," answered Mr. Pop.

Danny was **baffled**. "And how is that going to help me?" he asked **anxiously**. He already knew he would **dislike** the answer, but he asked the question anyway.

"A week at that camp will give you many more **disturbing nightmares**. So **dreadful** that you won't even remember the one with the hairy armpits ..." said his dad with a **smirk**.

Danny said **sarcastically**, "Ha, ha, very funny. I thought your job was to **appease** me, not add to my **anxiety**."

Mr. Pop ended the conversation **abruptly**, "You will be **appeased** when you get to camp and see that there is nothing to be worried about. Now, let's all get on the bus."

Fabulous, thought Danny as he squeezed through the crowded bus. The bus was full and all the passengers who had not **fainted** were able to find a cozy seat. But not Danny. He was the last one to get off the plane and onto the bus. He could barely find enough room to stand. *This trip is getting more and more **unappealing**, said Danny to himself. I cannot imagine anything worse than standing on a bus after such a long flight.*

"Excuse me," said a familiar voice behind him. "I think you dropped your passport." Danny turned around. Behind him was the owner of the hairy armpits handing him his passport. Danny smiled, took the passport, and decided not to take another breath for as long as he lived.

CHAPTER 3

The Departure

Luckily, the drive to the gate was very short. As soon as the bus stopped and opened its doors, several passengers popped out of the bus like confetti on New Year's Eve. Behind them, Danny was fighting for his life pushing and shoving people just to get a breath of fresh air.

"That's the spirit!" said Mr. Pop behind him. "I knew you were **eager** to go to camp! I was **certain** you would love the idea!"

"I am **eager**… to survive…," gasped Danny in **anguish**. "Please take me to the camp. I'm **certain** it will be more **appealing** than riding this bus. How can anyone stand such a smell?"

"It looks like you already started your adventure," said his mom, laughing hard as she **approached** her son. "Learning how to survive in **hostile environments** makes you stronger. However, I bet you'll like the camp **environment** better."

"I can't imagine there is an **environment** out there more **hostile** than the one on this bus. In fact, I'm **certain** the camp **environment** is more **appealing**," said Danny as he followed his parents into the airport.

After they passed through border control and got their luggage, the Pop family started looking for the driver that was supposed to meet them. Ten minutes later, there was still no sign of him.

"Where is the guy?" asked Mr. Pop **anxiously**. "He was supposed to meet us here with my name written on a board. I'm **certain** of that. I see plenty of names on boards, but not mine."

"Unless your name is *dod*..." said Danny, trying to be funny. He was pointing to a board held by a man who had been **adjacent** to them for the last ten minutes. "What kind of name is *dod* anyway?" Danny asked, **oblivious** to the fact that he had just solved the mystery of the missing driver.

"That's our name!" replied Mr. Pop happily. Danny was **baffled**. Mr. Pop **approached** the man who was holding the board and said, "Excuse me, but isn't this board upside down?"

"Oh, silly me! Of course. Are you Mr. Pop?"

"Yes, we are the Pop family, and this is Danny. Are you the driver?"

"Oh, no. I am Dutchee, the camp director. There has been a slight change of plans. We are leaving for the camp earlier than expected, so the bus loaded with all the kids is right here outside the airport. Danny, are you ready for a great adventure?"

"Yes, sure...I guess..." mumbled Danny.

"Then let's go!" said Dutchee.

The bus was indeed, right outside the airport. Danny hopped in and found a seat near the window. He was finally feeling a little bit more **appeased** with the idea of going to the camp. He even smiled and waved at his parents. He actually started to like the **environment** on this new bus. It was **certainly** less **hostile** than the **environment** on the other bus. The kids seemed normal. They had regularly-shaped teeth and there were no funny smells. Maybe his parents were right. He might even like this camp.

Mr. and Mrs. Pop waved back at their son. They were **appeased**, too. "Finally, our son is not **anxious** anymore," said Mr. Pop as he and his wife turned around and **approached** a taxi. They started busily loading their luggage into the taxi, **oblivious** to the fact that Dutchee had just boarded the bus followed by another passenger. **Oblivious** to the fact that the other passenger's hairy armpits were very familiar to Danny. **Oblivious** to the fact that, as the bus started to move, their son's **anguished** face was glued to the window. If they had looked back, they would have seen that his **hostile** looks were far from **appeasing**.

CHAPTER 4

The Bird's Nest

The bus full of kids was fast **approaching** Daris Camp. Almost two hours had passed since they had left the airport.

"What are you doing with your head outside the window?" asked a girl who was sitting on the seat **adjacent** to Danny's.

"I like the smell of fresh air. It is so … so fresh!" said Danny.

"I **agree**. My dog likes to do the same. Except that he also sticks his tongue out. You remind me of my dog. I like you."

"Thank you... I guess!" yelled Danny. He was a little **baffled**. He was not **certain** this was a **compliment**. He wanted to think that it was. After all, it sounded like she loved her dog. But Danny didn't feel very **grateful** about being compared to a dog.

"He also has fuzzy hair, just like you," continued the girl.

"I don't have fuzzy hair!" yelled Danny.

"Oh, you do, trust me. You've had your head hanging out of the window for almost an hour. I'm sure your new hairstyle will attract a lot of birds."

"What? What do you mean?" asked Danny, **baffled**. He decided to bring his head back inside the bus.

"Well, it looks just like a bird's nest. Wait, I think I see an egg... don't move."

Danny started to hit his head **ferociously** with both hands. Then he banged his head on the seat several times and shook it repeatedly before noticing the girl's **smirk**.

"Gotcha!" she said finally. "Oh, you are so **gullible**! Now I like you even more."

"I'm not a volleyball!" yelled Danny **exasperated**. This trip was becoming more and more **unappealing** by the minute. "And I dislike when people make fun of me!"

"Oh, no, not *volleyball*! I said, **gullible**. That describes people who believe almost everything they are told," explained the girl. "I didn't mean to make fun of you... It's just that your hair is so..."

"Nesty?" Danny finished her sentence. They both started to giggle.

"Ok, I admit that I'm a bit **gullible** and my hair looks like a bird's nest. But I feel more **grateful** when people pay me **compliments**".

"Hmmm... let me see. I think I have one **compliment** for you..."

"Attention everyone!" Dutchee's voice interrupted the conversation between the two kids. "We will arrive at the camp in just a few minutes. As soon as you get off the bus and **retrieve** your luggage, you will find your name and your room number at the camp's main entrance. The rooms are unlocked. Let the fun begin!"

As soon as Dutchee finished talking, the bus stopped **abruptly**. It appeared that the driver had almost missed the entrance to the camp.

"We're here!" exclaimed the girl. "By the way, my name is Lucy. Everybody calls me Lucy, except for my mother who occasionally calls me Lucy Diana Moldovan. When she does that, I'm in trouble. That means she is **exasperated** by me. OK, see you!" And she took off.

"But what about my **compliment**?" asked Danny.

"Wait a minute! I know you," said a familiar voice behind Danny. Danny didn't have to turn around to know who was talking. The smell of the hairy armpits was already **dreadful** and made him **eager** to disappear. He pretended not to hear the comment.

"Lucy Diana Moldovan, wait for me!!!"

CHAPTER 5

Daris Camp

Daris Camp was a much nicer place than Danny had **predicted**. It was a **remote** location, far from the heavy **rush hour** traffic of a big city and **adjacent** to a forest. It had several **sparse** wood cabins that looked very tidy and welcoming. A river with crystal-clear water flowed nearby, and Danny thought that he saw an **enormous** fish swimming **swiftly** down the river. Or was it a shadow? Of what?

Danny's **anguish** slowly died down, and he started to feel at **ease** again. As it turned out, the owner of the hairy armpits was not joining them at the camp. She had left with the bus, and Danny **assumed** that she was just a tourist in need of a ride. He was **grateful** now to breathe the **pervasively** fresh air. He had to admit: he could not get enough of it!

The fresh air was not the only thing **pervasive** in this **environment.** There was also a **pervasive** happy feeling throughout the whole camp. All the kids seemed friendly and excited to be there. A counselor named Christina, welcomed them with a wide smile and showed them around the camp. The children were super excited, especially when they saw the fabulous game room!

Andreea, another counselor, told the children all about the fun-filled program for the week. They couldn't be more thrilled when they heard about things like cave exploration and a white water rafting trip. Last, the children met Dorin in the archery section of the camp. He was the counselor responsible for the outdoor activities, and the children knew immediately that they would have a fantastic time with him when they saw the **enormous** ropes course. As much as he had insisted otherwise to his parents, Danny now had to **agree** that he did not dislike the camp. He was **eager** to start the activities and was **certain** that he would have a **fabulous** time after all.

After the tour of the camp, Danny went to check out his one-room cabin. The room was neat and had two bunk beds. *I wonder who my roommate is...* Danny's thoughts were interrupted **abruptly** by a voice behind him.

"Is this cabin number eight? I hope it's number eight. My bags are so heavy! I couldn't move them one inch further if I tried! Please tell me this is cabin number eight!"

Danny turned around and saw a short boy with curly hair and sparkling eyes.

"Yes, this is cabin number eight..." Danny replied. He wanted to introduce himself, but the boy zoomed right past him.

"Ooh, ooh, look! Bunk beds! I'll take the top bed. Can I take the top bunk? Please? I want the top bunk. I can't stand the smell of my shoes. I need to sleep as far away as possible from them. Here, sniff."

The boy took his shoes off and shoved them in Danny's face. Danny tried to be polite and said, "They smell great. They smell like soap."

"Eew..." the boy made an **anguished** face. "Do you have a soap that smells like shoes? I feel really badly for you, brother. Can I take the top bed?"

"I **assume** you're my roommate. What's your name?" asked Danny.

"I'm Alex," the boy finally introduced himself.

"Alex, it's nice to meet you. I'll be happy to let you have the top bunk but promise me that you will never make anybody smell your shoes again."

"Deal!"

The two boys continued their conversation as they unpacked their bags. They learned that they both had just finished sixth grade, they both had come to this camp because their parents made them, and they were both scared of vampires. Alex decided to put his shoes outside, on the front porch, to keep vampires away. Alex was **certain** that the smell would stop any living creature from getting close to the cabin. That made the two boys feel more at **ease**... so much at **ease** that they forgot to lock their door.

As the sun was **swiftly** setting, the boys were getting sleepy. Their conversation was soon replaced by mumbling sounds. The mumbling sounds were replaced by wheezing sounds, and the wheezing sounds were replaced by snores. The snoring symphony made it clear that both boys were completely **oblivious** to the moving shadow by their window. **Oblivious** to the lowered door handle and to the fact that their unlocked door was starting to open. **Oblivious** to what was about to happen.

CHAPTER 6

Monday

The first day at Daris Camp dawned peacefully. The chirping of the birds and the **soothing** sounds of the nearby river were very enjoyable. There was no other sound that morning... except for a **ferocious** scream that woke everybody up.

"AAAAAHHHH!"

The first scream was immediately followed by a **dreadful shriek**, and then the two screams were combined to create a choir of terrifying yells.

"AAAAAAAAAAAAAAAAHHHHHHHHHHHHHH!"

Everybody at Daris Camp opened their doors and windows to see what was happening. The **shrieks** were coming from cabin number eight. A few seconds later, Danny and Alex **hurtled** from their cabin and started to run **chaotically** around the camp. They were getting dangerously close to the river.

"AAAAHHHH! Blood! You have blood on your face! Look at your face! Blood! Blood!!" Danny was both **shrieking** and **shivering** out of fear as he ran run around in circles, pointing to Alex's face.

"AAAAAHHHH! Your neck! Your neck! The two red dots! Look! You've been bitten by a vampire! A vampire! This is not happening!" Alex slapped himself **ferociously**, thinking that it might help him wake up from this **nightmare**. It did not work. He was already awake.

Christina's cabin was nearby. When she heard the screams, she **hurtled** outside and ran towards the boys to try to calm them down. That turned out to be a bad idea. When the two boys saw her, they started to **shriek** and **shiver** even louder. Then they grabbed onto each other and jumped straight into the **frigid** river. Luckily, the water was only two feet deep.

Dutchee showed up just in time to end the **chaos**. "Oh, I see you boys are getting ready for the rafting adventure," he said. "Now, stop all this non-sense. After you wash that jam off your faces, get some dry clothes on and go to the cafeteria. Breakfast is in twenty minutes."

"J-J-Jam?" asked Danny, **shivering** from the cold water. "Jam? Alex's face is covered with jam? Do you mean that if I wipe his face like this... and taste the... hmmm, strawberry! This is **delicious**!"

"What about the marks on your neck?" Alex asked Danny.

Danny used his fingers to wipe the two dots off his neck and then tasted them. "Yup! Still strawberry!"

"What about Christina?" asked Alex.

"What about Christina?" asked Dutchee. Then he looked over at the camp counselor and started to laugh.

"What about me?" asked Christina.

"What about Christina?" yelled the two boys, still **shivering**.

"It looks like Christina was putting on her lipstick when she heard you scream," explained Dutchee.

"Yes, I was...Wait a minute, how did you know that?" asked Christina.

"I **assume** the **shrieks** took you by surprise," continued Dutchee. "Your hand shook, and you drew a red mark on your face with the lipstick. The mark is running down from the corner of your mouth, and now you look like a vampire who has just finished drinking someone's blood! I'm sure there was nothing **soothing** about you running towards the boys when they thought they had just been bitten by a vampire."

As the boys climbed out of the water, Dutchee turned to them and continued, "This is **typical**. It looks like someone played a prank on you. We'll find out who did it. In the future, make sure you lock your door at night. Now, go change your clothes quickly. The water is **frigid**."

Fabulous! No, this is not your **typical** *Monday morning,* thought Danny as he and Alex returned to their cabin. *It's* **typical** *to take a shower in the morning and it's* **typical** *to eat* **delicious** *strawberry jam for breakfast. But not like this!*

CHAPTER 7

The Compliments

Breakfast started at eight o'clock sharp. Danny and Alex were **determined** to ignore everybody who was looking at them and whispering behind their back. Which was pretty much everybody in the cafeteria.

"Hello, bird's nest!" Lucy took her plate and joined the two boys. "Are you here for seconds?"

"Excuse me?" said Danny.

"I thought you already had breakfast in the middle of the river. I bet the strawberry jam was **delicious**. But it seems that your **appetite** did not **diminish**, and you need more food."

"Ha-ha, very funny!" said Danny **sarcastically**. "I see you're **determined** to make people feel badly."

"No, actually, I'm here to pay you a **compliment**. I owe you one - remember? Here it goes: I think you two are the fastest people in this camp. I don't think there's anybody else here who could jump in the **frigid** water that **swiftly**. If they had a contest to see how

swiftly could people jump in the water, I'm sure you'd win."

"Of course we would, because we'd be the only ones crazy enough to actually jump in that water. Do you have any idea how **frigid** it is?" asked Alex.

"I can tell from your blue lips. By the way, I'm Lucy."

"I'm Alex. Danny's roommate. It's nice to meet you."

"You too. Now, here's a secret about this place…"

The two boys leaned toward her, **eager** to find out what secrets she might **reveal**.

"YOU MUST BE REALLY STUPID TO THINK THAT VAMPIRES ARE REAL!" Lucy yelled in their ears.

"Does she owe you any more **compliments**?" Alex asked Danny, his voice dripping with **sarcasm**.

"No, this **compliment** was a bonus," replied Danny.

"Just think about it, guys", continued Lucy. "When the other kids see you being so **gullible** and realize that you believe all the stories you hear about vampires, it will be very easy for anyone to **deceive** you and play pranks on you. Stop acting so scared of vampires. This **environment** is not as **hostile** as you think."

"That's easy for you to say," mumbled Alex. "When somebody is **determined** to come at night…"

"Wait! I just heard something fall under the table. Alex, I think it belongs to you," interrupted Lucy.

"What? What is it?" asked Alex. He **swiftly** dived under the table.

"It's your COURAGE my **gullible** new friend. Pick it up and never lose it again!" said Lucy **exasperated**. "Where is your **appetite** for adventure?"

"Why do you even care about us?" asked Danny.

"OK, I'm about to **reveal** another secret to you," said Lucy.

When they heard her mention another secret, Danny and Alex moved away

from her, ready to cover their ears. But Lucy's voice was much **diminished** this time. She whispered, "I just found out that we'll be together on the same rafting team. I also heard that the winning team gets a **delicious**, **enormous** cake at dinner. I don't know about you guys, but I'm **determined** to win that cake."

"Is it a strawberry cake?" asked Alex, and they all started giggling.

CHAPTER 8

The Training

After breakfast, all the children met the camp counselors by the river. They were divided into four groups, and each group was led to their raft by one of the counselors. Lucy was right. She and the two boys were on the same team, together with four other kids.

"Listen up, boys and girls!" shouted Dorin, their team leader. "Before you **hurtle** over the waves in a raft, you need to have **suitable** training, and that's what we're going to do next. This trip will be long, and you need to be prepared. It is **crucial** that all of you work as a team and follow directions **properly**. When I tell you to paddle, you don't pick your nose: you paddle! When I tell you to paddle, you don't pick your friend's nose: YOU PADDLE! Rafting takes

team effort to **succeed,** and you will **diminish** our chances of winning if you are not doing what you're supposed to do. It is **crucial** that you work together to **succeed**."

Dorin **retrieved** a paddle from the raft and showed everybody how to use it **properly**. Then, he **retrieved** more paddles and gave one to each kid, letting them practice the moves before they got in the raft. While the kids paddled through an imaginary river, Dorin equipped each of them with **suitable** helmets and **suitable** life jackets. Then, he **retrieved** a map from his pocket and gathered everyone around him.

"We are here and we will paddle all the way to this place," he said pointing to two areas on the map. "The first **section** is easy to handle. We only have a few **sparse** rocks to avoid. Then, as we **approach** the mid-**section** of the river, the water will be **swifter**. At that time, you will see an island that splits the river in two. It is **crucial** that we keep left. The river is not as **swift** on that side, and it is **predictable**."

"What will happen if we turn right?" asked Alex, visibly **disturbed**. "What will happen? Has anyone survived rafting that route? Is it **dreadful**? Are we going to drown? I DON'T WANT TO DROWN!"

"If we turn right, the route will be **chaotic** and the water will be **ferocious**," said the counselor. "That **section** is not for beginners, but the water is not deep. The route is just **swift** and bumpy. Don't worry, Alex. Just follow my lead and you'll be fine. As I said, it is **crucial** to be a team player."

"But what if we get lost? Can we get lost? What if we get stuck?" insisted Alex.

"If we get lost or stuck, I will call Dutchee and he will send out a rescue team. See, I have my cell phone right here in my pocket," said Dorin. "Any other questions?"

"When do we eat?" asked Alex.

"I have snacks for everyone in my backpack. That will be your lunch. We'll eat as soon as the trip is over. We'll be back at the camp by dinnertime. Anything else?" continued Dorin.

"How is the last **section** of the river?" asked Danny.

"The river is much calmer in the last **section**. We will paddle until we see an **enormous** bus parked near the banks of the river. That will be the end of our route. I will help you guide the raft to the shore. The bus driver will **retrieve** the rafts and take us back to the camp. He will also mark the time of our arrival. Since Dutchee is recording the time of our departure (we will pass by him in a minute), we'll be able to find out which team was the **swiftest**. As you probably know, an **enormous**, **delicious** cake will be given to the winning team. So, let's have a win!"

The children were thrilled. Their **appetite** for adventure was now enhanced by an **appetite** for cake. Everybody wanted to win this contest! The kids **hurtled** into the raft and each found a **proper** spot. They were ready to go!

The rafts of the other teams left one by one. The raft led by Dorin left last.

"Ready or not, here we come!" yelled Dorin enthusiastically as he launched the raft into the water. He yelled so loudly that he did not hear his cell phone falling out of his pocket and into the river.

CHAPTER 9

The Distraction

The rafting **endeavor** began. All the children paddled as Dorin instructed them, and the ride was as smooth as **predicted**. A few **sparse** rocks were sticking out of the water, but the team **succeeded** at avoiding them with **ease**.

The trip offered the children the chance to see a fabulous **environment** just beyond the banks of the river. They were **fascinated** when they spotted the ruins of a castle and they were surprised when they saw a trout jumping out of the water to catch an insect.

"Look, look! A big bird!" yelled Alex, **fascinated**, as he stood up and pointed his finger up in the air.

"Alex, sit down and paddle!" said Dorin firmly.

"But that bird is **enormous**! It's the biggest bird I've ever seen in my life!" insisted Alex, waving his paddle in the air.

"Alex, sit down! It's not safe to stand up and wave the paddle like that!" yelled Dorin.

"Look! The bird is coming this way! Wait – is this bird friendly?" Alex had a sudden feeling of **anguish**.

"Sit down! You might hurt somebody!" yelled Dorin **exasperated**. He leaned towards Alex and tried to pull him down. At the same time, Alex **abruptly** turned around and **accidentally** hit Dorin in the forehead with his paddle.

Plop! In an instant, Dorin fell overboard while the raft continued floating down the river. The shock of the **accidental** hit and the contact with the **frigid** water knocked Dorin out for several seconds. He did not actually **faint**, but by the time he realized what had just happened, his chances of catching up to the raft were very **remote**.

It's all right. They will be fine, Dorin tried to convince himself as he swam to shore. *I'll just make a call, and Dutchee will take care of this*. As he reached his hand into his empty pocket, hoping to **retrieve** his phone, Dorin started to **shiver**. He had just realized that his phone was missing and all the kids in his raft were now on their own. Nobody knew that they would need stopping the raft at the meeting point. Who knew where they might end up? He looked around. There was nobody he could ask for help. His hope **diminished** by the minute. This **endeavor** had **certainly** not gone according to the plan.

CHAPTER 10

On Their Own

After a few moments of confusion, the kids started to panic, shouting and waving their arms **chaotically**.

"AAAAAHHHHHHH!!!!!"

Their **ferocious shrieks** scared the daylight out of every living creature within a mile. The only one to **soothe** the other children's **anxiety** and say something **intelligible** was Lucy.

"Guys, yelling your lungs out won't help steer the raft in the right direction. We will **succeed** only if we work as a team. So grab your paddles and stop knocking people off the raft!"

"It was an **accident**!" Alex insisted. He began sobbing.

"We know that," Danny tried to **appease** him. "I'm sure Dorin is fine – he's a grown up. Now, let's make him proud and finish this **endeavor**. Our training was **adequate**. I'm sure we can still win that **delicious** cake."

"Look – the island!" yelled Lucy. "This is where we're supposed to turn left, right?"

"Right…" said Danny in **disbelief**. "Right!" yelled all the kids in the raft. As they **approached** the island, they started paddling towards the right side of the island.

"What are you doing?" yelled Lucy. "We're supposed to turn left, right?"

"Yes, we're turning right!" said Alex.

The raft was **swiftly** veering right.

"No, you're turning right!" said Lucy, **exasperated**.

"Yes, we're turning right," said one of the kids. "That's what you just said we should do!"

"No, I said you should turn LEFT!" yelled Lucy.

"You're not being **intelligible**, Lucy! Make up your mind. Is it left, or right?" said Danny, completely **baffled**.

"Left! Left!" yelled Lucy.

All the kids tried to turn the raft **abruptly** in the other direction, but their task was difficult. They just did not have **adequate** power.

"Nevermind…it's too late now," said Danny, as he and all the other kids watched the island passing on their left. "We're already on the second **section** of our trip. The rough one!"

"Are you saying that we've taken the deadly route?" asked

31

Alex in **disbelief**. "Is that what you're saying?"

"I'm saying we should all brace ourseeeeeeeeelves!" said Danny as the raft **swiftly** increased its speed.

"Mommy! I will miss you, Mommy!" wailed Alex. "I'm sorry for **accidentally** dropping gum in your shoes! I'm sorry for sneezing on your sandwich when you weren't paying attention! I'm sooo...".

Suddenly, a **ferocious** rumble stopped Alex's whining. The raft bounced off a huge rock and started to spin as the kids held on to each other for dear life, yelling even harder.

CHAPTER 11

The Return of the **Ingested** Food

The group hug lasted for what seemed an **eternity**.

"Guys, I think I'm going to be sick," said Lucy after a while.

"No!" yelled all the other kids.

"My stomach can't handle this anymore," she continued. Her words were anything but **soothing**.

"Tell your stomach that we're not interested in your **ingested** food and that he should stay busy doing his job," **suggested** Danny, **shivering** at the idea of Lucy's vomit spraying **pervasively** around the raft.

"My stomach thanks you for your **suggestion**, but he says he is not interested in *your* interests," said Lucy. "My food **typically** comes up if I spin for a long time after I have breakfast," she **revealed**.

"It's just **fascinating** hearing what your stomach has to **reveal**," said one of the kids **sarcastically**. "However, might you **suggest** to your stomach that he keeps your **ingested** food down just a little bit longer? We'd all be **grateful**," he added with a **smirk**.

"The spinning won't last an **eternity**," added Danny, trying to **appease** Lucy. She gave him a look of utter **disbelief**.

"What makes you **assume** that?" she asked as she became paler than a vampire. "Oh, no. I think...it's coming..."

Then, it happened. An **enormous** amount of vomit ended up in Alex's lap.

"Eww! Seriously?" yelled Alex. "Ewww! This is gross! Ewww! Couldn't this day get any worse?" he complained, getting up and trying to clean himself off.

Danny tried to **suggest** that anything was possible (and yes, it could – and would - get much worse than this) when the raft **abruptly** hit an **enormous**, sharp-looking rock. They all heard a loud noise, followed by water rushing into the raft. The kids all saw how quickly the raft started to **deteriorate**. They also saw Alex struggling to keep his balance. He did not **succeed**. Instead, he fell off the raft just as Danny was reaching out to grab him.

"I got him! I got him!" yelled Danny. He yanked back his hand, but all that he was able to rescue were Alex's shorts and underwear.

CHAPTER 12

The Landing

Soon, the **deteriorated** raft reached the muddy banks of the river. Luckily, the water there was shallow, and all the kids got off the raft safely. Alex was safe, too, although he was hiding far away from the group, behind the sharp-looking rock. He was not **grateful** to Danny for leaving him without his underwear.

"Lucy, you need to start doing a better job of chewing your food! Look at this chunk of bread!" said Danny, pointing to Alex's shorts that were laying on the ground. They were still covered with Lucy's vomit.

"Uh, guys? I'm okay, don't worry about me!" yelled Alex **sarcastically** from behind the rock. "Now, can I have my clothes back?"

"I'm not touching those again!" said Danny.

"Danny, I need my clothes!" Alex **grumbled** from behind the rock. He was becoming **enraged**.

"Why? They are **deteriorated**," said Danny.

"They are not **deteriorated**!" Alex was getting more and more **enraged**. "They are only dirty. Give me back my clothes! I'm turning into a popsicle in this **frigid** water."

Danny used a long stick to **retrieve** Alex's clothes. Holding his nose with his free hand, he walked towards Alex. Only a few steps before reaching him, Danny **accidentally** slipped on a wet rock and lost his balance. He also lost control of the stick and dropped  it in the water. Alex watched in **disbelief** as his clothes were **swiftly** taken by the rushing water of their river and disappeared. What a **dreadful nightmare**!

"Oops," whispered Danny, while Alex **grumbled** something **unintelligible**. Whatever he said, it was probably not a **compliment**.

"Is everybody okay down there?" a loud voice thundered behind them. A man **approached** the group of kids.

"Some of us more than others," giggled Lucy.

"How did you get here so fast?" he asked. "You were supposed to **arrive** much later."

"Are you the bus driver that was supposed to meet us at the end of the trip and **retrieve** our raft?" asked Danny.

"You bet I am. You've reached your final destination. My bus is ready to pick up you and your... **deteriorated** raft," he added. "Let me get you some clean and dry clothes. I guess I'll start with the naked guy behind that rock."

All the kids, excluding Alex, were very happy that their rafting **endeavor** had ended well. And as they were waiting for the other teams to **arrive**, their **appetites** started to increase. They had won the cake!

CHAPTER 13

Exhaustion

The kids riding the bus back to camp were completely **depleted** of energy. Their rafting **endeavor** had been fun but **exhausting**. Their muscles started to feel sore one by one ... they had no idea that their bodies had so many muscles!

When the bus **arrived** at the camp, the kids were welcomed by... Dorin! He had **succeeded** in hiking his way back to camp! Dorin watched his team get off the bus in **disbelief**. Amazingly, they had handled the remaining **sections** of the trip all by themselves! The kids were thrilled to see Dorin safe. They all came together in a group hug and tried to share their stories. With everyone speaking at once, they were **unintelligible**. Eventually, Dorin learned that his team had won first place and the **delicious** cake! He felt so proud of them!

That evening, the kids from Dorin's team **depleted** their dinner plates **swiftly**. They were **exhausted** but starving! The day's **endeavor** had given each of them an **enormous appetite**. Dorin's fall into the water with their snacks had **certainly** not helped, either. Lucy in particular was very **grateful** to have a **proper** meal since she had left most of her breakfast on Alex's shorts. When the cake **arrived**, the kids were drooling. It looked very **appealing**! The campers **hurtled** themselves towards the cake **chaotically**, attacking it with their forks before any of the instructors could say anything. When all was said and done, they **ingested** the cake in less than a minute.

Danny and Alex returned to their cabin dragging their feet. They were **exhausted**, too. All they wanted was an **adequate** night's sleep. Despite their **exhaustion**, they remembered to lock the door before they went to bed. To be on the safe side, they stacked all the furniture they could find in the cabin against the door. It was **crucial** that they had a long, **soothing** sleep after such a wild **endeavor**. They were **determined** to keep the **deceitful** prankster away from them. They were **determined** to keep the strawberry jam off their faces.

CHAPTER 14

Tuesday

Tuesday morning was a **pleasant** one for everybody at Daris Camp. There were no frantic **shrieks disturbing** the serene **environment**. Christina **succeeded** in **properly** applying her lipstick on her lips, and not on her face. Nobody jumped in the river that morning, and nobody tasted strawberry jam from his roommate's face.

Danny and Alex woke up well rested. They were **pleasantly** surprised to **notice** that nobody had entered their room during the night. The boys went to breakfast, but their muscles were so sore that their forks could barely find the way to their mouths.

"I'm **grateful** we're not leaving the camp today," said Danny. "I'm **exhausted**!"

"Me too. That rafting trip was **ferocious**!" replied Alex.

"Good morning, Danny. Is your face covered with transparent strawberry jam today? I **notice** you don't seem to be wearing any this morning. Oh, Alex. Hello to you too! I almost didn't recognize you with your pants on," Lucy greeted the two boys **sarcastically**.

"Lucy, where do you go to school, anyway? Is it called **Compliment** Elementary?" asked Danny.

"Is that where you were taught to be so **pleasant** to others?" added Alex with sarcasm.

"I'm sorry guys, I can't help it," Lucy tried to **appease** them. "Yesterday's **events** were just too **hilarious**!"

"I **agree** they were **hilarious**... to you!" **grumbled** Alex. "I'm sure you would be **enraged** if people **depleted** the contents of their stomach on your pants," he added.

"Hey, at least I didn't have a big breakfast," Lucy replied, trying to **diminish** his **anguish**. "The good news is that today we have Field Day at Daris Camp. I **assume** these **events** will be less **chaotic**, right?"

"Right," Alex **grumbled** in **disbelief**.

"Nothing bad should happen," continued Lucy. "Except maybe when we ride the zip-line."

"What?!" Alex jumped off his seat, suddenly **shivering** with fear. "What are you talking about? What zip-line? I don't like heights!"

"Oh, you're so **gullible**! **Settle** down, my crybaby friend," said Lucy. "You won't ride the zip-line…" she started to explain with a **smirk** on her face.

"Phew! Don't scare me like that again!" said Alex.

"…because you'll **faint** before that **event**, during the worm-eating contest," she continued. Then Lucy took off, leaving Alex more **baffled** than ever.

He had suddenly lost his **appetite**.

CHAPTER 15

A Snack in the Woods

The Field Day **events** did not seem as **dreadful** as Lucy had **suggested** they would be. Alex and Danny learned that they would do a variety of fun outdoor activities, such as a scavenger hunt and a worm eating competition. Yes, they would have to **ingest** worms... CANDY worms, to be more **precise**. Lucy had **deceived** them again! Well, they had to admit she had actually told them the truth about eating worms, but she had let them **assume** that the **events** would be extremely **unpleasant**.

For the scavenger hunt, the children had to **retrieve** well-hidden **items** spread **sparsely** throughout the forest **adjacent** to the camp. They didn't know what **items** they were looking for, but they were given some clues. Once they found the correct **item**, a note attached to it would give them clues to their next discovery.

The kids' first clue **suggested** that they search in a clearing for something resembling a fist-sized, dark-colored egg. They searched and searched for what seemed an **eternity** when Alex **noticed** something matching that description in the grass.

"I found it!" he **shrieked**. He ran happily towards Danny, squeezing the **item** in his hand. "Danny, look! I found it!" he said proudly.

"Alex, this is poop," said Danny. "Cow poop, to be more **precise**."

"Eew!" Alex threw it away and wiped his hands on the front of his shirt.

"Great!" **grumbled** Danny. "Now this smell will follow us everywhere. You'd better wash your shirt before you get back to our cabin."

"Oops, sorry! I wasn't thinking **properly**," said Alex.

"Guys, can you guess what the first **item** is?" Lucy **approached** the two boys. "It's a chocolate egg wrapped in dark-colored... eew, what is that smell?"

"It's Alex. He didn't have time to shower this morning," said Danny trying to **diminish** the **embarrassment** of his friend.

"Dude, soap is good for you. Anyway, can you guess how I know?" continued Lucy.

"Did you have a **nightmare** last night where you were chased by chocolate eggs?" asked Danny.

"No…" Lucy paused to add dramatic effect to her statement before exclaiming, "I found it!" Lucy **revealed** a chocolate egg that was tucked neatly in her pocket. She tried to **appease** the boys by sharing it with them.

"I'm sorry for being **sarcastic** with you this morning," she said. She then crushed the egg into smaller pieces and gave one piece to each boy.

"Apology accepted!" said Alex, clapping his hands. He was very hungry since he hadn't eaten much of his breakfast.

"What do you know? Miss **Compliment** Elementary knows how to be **pleasant** sometimes," added Danny.

The three kids quickly **ingested** their pieces of chocolate. Then, they let the other kids know that they had found the **item**. Everyone was so jealous! And now they were even more **determined** to find the next **item**!

The second clue said that the kids should look for multiple small **items** near a big tree, about 150 steps away from where they were. The kids spread out in all different directions looking for them.

Danny and Alex walked past a large tree when Alex **noticed** several small, round **items** that looked like chocolate candy. He **shrieked** again.

"Danny, I found them!" He grabbed a couple in his hand and said, "Wait, is this cow poop?"

"No…" said Danny.

"Great! Because I'm starving!" continued Alex as he tossed them in his mouth.

"It's sheep poop," added Danny.

CHAPTER 16

A **Solitary** Shepherd

When you visit **rural** Transylvania, you often meet shepherds. Shepherds tend the sheep all day, making sure they are safe. They live a **solitary** life, which means they spend most of their time alone. Sometimes they get bored without much **entertainment** out in the fields. However, many shepherds enjoy their **solitary** way of life because they get to spend their time outdoors.

On the morning of the scavenger hunt, a shepherd was sitting by the river **adjacent** to Daris Camp. He was enjoying the cool shade of a pine tree and the **typical** quietness of his **rural environment**. His sheep stood in a shallow **section** of the river, drinking water. Suddenly, he saw a little boy running out of the woods. A second boy followed him in a **rush**. *Typical*, the shepherd thought. *These city boys act like it's **rush hour** everywhere, even in **rural** areas.*

When the first boy **arrived** at the river, he jumped in without hesitation.

"Alex, are you alright?" the other boy asked. But Alex did not reply. He dipped his head into the water and pulled it back out **swiftly**.

Then he then took a mouthful of the clear water and spat it back into the river. Next, he took another mouthful of water and began to **gargle**. Finally, he spat it back out again.

The shepherd was **baffled**. *These city boys are crazy! They must not know that when you want to drink water, you swallow it – you don't spit it out!*

Next, Alex took a rock and scrubbed his tongue with it. He scrubbed it over and over again until his tongue started to bleed. He swallowed another mouthful of water, **gargled** for another ten seconds, then spat it back out.

The shepherd was **fascinated**. For him, this was far from a typical Tuesday. He had not had this much **entertainment** in a very long time. This boy was **hilarious**. *Who uses rocks to scrub their tongues, anyway? I bet this is a new habit the city folks have. I'll never move into the city*, the shepherd thought as he **approached** the two boys.

"Young men, around here when we want to take a bath, we use

a pond. It's not very far. The water is clean and warm," the shepherd said.

Alex and Danny froze for a second. They had been **oblivious** to the fact that someone was watching them.

"Oh no, sir," Danny tried to save his friend from **embarrassment**. Again. "My friend Alex loves taking baths in this river."

"Yes, the water is very **pleasant** and clean! I love the taste of this water. It's **delicious**," added Alex with a wide smile.

"I don't know about that…" said the shepherd a bit **baffled**. "You see, my sheep are taking a bath too, not far from here. I wouldn't put water in my mouth that has also washed my dirty sheep. Besides, if I were you, I would get out of that **frigid** water before I caught a cold," **suggested** the shepherd.

"Actually, the water is not **frigid**," Alex said, trying to save himself from even further **embarrassment**. "It's **pleasantly** warm," he added.

"Oh, well, that means my sheep must be peeing in it," said the shepherd.

Alex's smile disappeared. He felt that he was about to **faint**.

CHAPTER 17

Discreet

"Dude, that was **disgusting**," said Danny as he and Alex were walking back to cabin number eight. Alex needed to change his clothes, and Danny was there to support him.

"You think?" replied Alex **sarcastically**. He was **shivering ferociously** from the chock of the cold water and the sheep incident.

"Hey, at least you didn't actually **ingest** any of the sheep poop or 'sheep soup'," Danny laughed, trying to **entertain** his friend.

"Let me just tell you something," Alex defended himself with **stoicism**. He was working hard to keep calm and not show any emotion. "That sheep soup was organic. No chemicals, no artificial flavors... Served fresh... An original recipe... A wonderful... unique... uh... uh..." Suddenly, Alex lost all his **stoicism** and burst into tears wailing loud enough to scare all the living creatures in the forest. "Who am I kidding?!??! That was seriously **disgusting**!!!"

"Don't worry, my friend. You don't have to explain anything to me. I'll be **discreet**," replied Danny.

"De-de-delete?" Alex was still **shivering** and had to work hard to talk **intelligibly**. "Danny, h-how can you delete all that happened?"

"I didn't say…" Danny paused for a second. "What happened when your head was under the water? Did fish lay eggs into your ears or something? I said **discreet**… you know, I'll be careful about what I say. I'll keep all this quiet and not share your story with others," explained Danny, trying to lessen his friend's **anxiety**.

"Don't share it with anybody! Nobody needs to know what happened, Danny! Nobody! Can you promise me that?" said Alex. He was feeling a little bit hopeful. Danny was his friend and his roommate, and Alex felt that he could trust him.

Danny made a pinky promise with him, and Alex felt his **stoicism** returning when he suddenly heard a loud voice behind them.

"Alex, what's happening? I thought I heard you crying!" It was Dutchee. He **approached** the two boys with a concerned look on his face.

"Oh, no, that was a song we just learned from a **solitary** shepherd," explained Alex.

"Yes, Alex loves campfire songs!" added Danny, **noticing** that Dutchee was not easily **deceived**. "He would like to **entertain** us by performing during the bonfire! He has a collection of weird songs! You'll be amazed by the sounds he can make."

"But why are you all wet, Alex?" insisted Dutchee. "What happened to you?"

"Oh, nothing **disgusting**!" Alex had become **stoic** once more and was now acting as if nothing **embarrassing** had ever happened. "I took a quick bath in the river and now I feel refreshed. I love the **rural** lifestyle!"

"Yes, and now we need to hurry before we miss the other activities," Danny ended the conversation **abruptly**. "See you later,

Dutchee!"

The two boys rushed towards their cabin before Dutchee could say anything more. They were hoping that the counselor would be **discreet** and not let any of the other kids know about their unusual meeting. After all, maybe he really was **gullible** enough to believe their story! Danny and Alex both felt a bit relieved.

"That was close... for a moment there, I thought he would discover my secret," Alex sighted. "Luckily, we are the only ones who know what happened."

"Um, are you absolutely sure about that?" asked Danny in **disbelief**. They had just arrived in front of their cabin when he **noticed** a bag hanging on the door handle. That was a very unusual sight. There was a note attached to the bag. That was even more unusual. Danny opened the note, and read it aloud: "Still hungry?"

"Oh, how nice!" said Alex. "Somebody brought us lunch." Then he opened the bag. It was filled with small brown **items** that looked like chocolate candy. Only they weren't chocolate, and they smelled terribly.

CHAPTER 18

The **Hypotheses**

"This is the most **embarrassing** day in the history of **embarrassing** days!" whined Alex. He had managed to change his clothes, and now he and Danny were rushing back to meet the other kids. Alex could not stop thinking about how **embarrassing** it would be if everybody in the camp discovered what had happened to him.

"I **assume** whoever did this just wants to play a prank on you," said Danny. "Since the person knows where our cabin is, my **hypothesis** is that it is the same person who put jam on our faces."

"My **hypothesis** is that your **hypothesis** is wrong!" said Alex. "I know it was somebody else."

"How?" asked Danny.

"I just know," insisted Alex. "I have a feeling."

"Well, my **hypothesis** about your **hypothesis** that my **hypothesis** is wrong is that you don't understand very well what a **hypothesis** is," said Danny. "A **hypothesis** is an educated **assumption**, or a guess. And the key word here is *educated*. That means you make a statement based on **evidence** that you already have, not based on a feeling."

Just then, the two boys **noticed** the other kids from the camp. They were scattered about **sparsely**, looking for fallen tree branches and making huts out of them. Nobody seemed to notice their **arrival**.

"Danny, listen to my new **hypothesis**," said Alex. "Since everybody looks so busy - and that is solid **evidence** - maybe nobody will notice that we were ever gone if we rejoin the group **discreetly**. We can pretend that we've been here all morning!"

"I like that plan," whispered Danny. "Let's sneak in! Grab that stick and act busy."

As the two boys began to **approach** the other kids, they suddenly heard an ear-piercing **shriek** coming from the group. It was Lucy. She was sitting on a log, calling their names.

"Danny! Alex! What happened to you, guys?"

With that, all the kids stopped looking for branches and turned around to see Danny and Alex trying to join the group **discreetly**. Lucy continued, "My butt fell asleep waiting for you on this log! Come and look what I found! I have plenty of chocolate eggs left for you! Wait…" She paused for a second and then she continued yelling. "Is everything okay with you? Why are you whispering to each other? And Alex, why are you wearing different clothes?"

Alex looked at Danny and whispered, "I have a new **hypothesis**. Based on the **evidence** that everybody is looking at us right now, and Lucy noticed I'm wearing different clothes, I **hypothesize** that it will be difficult to convince anybody that we have been here all morning."

Dorin approached the two boys, "Danny, Alex, we've been looking all over for you. Are you okay?"

"We totally are," Danny replied. "We're testing **hypotheses** and you just gave us solid evidence that supports one of them!"

"Oh, I'm glad I could help! Now, let's finish building these huts before lunchtime!"

CHAPTER 19

Suspicion

The huts were finished before lunchtime. The children returned to the camp and lined up in the cafeteria. Their appetite was **enormous**, and the food smelled so **delicious**!

Danny and Alex were waiting in line when Alex whispered to Danny, "I have a **suspicion**. I think I know who the prankster is."

"Who?" asked Danny **intrigued**.

"Do you see that boy in the green shirt? He's been staring at us for the past two minutes," answered Alex.

"How do you know it's him?" asked Danny. "Do you have any other **evidence**?"

"No, but why would anybody stare at us like that? It's very **suspicious**," insisted Alex.

The boy in the green shirt **approached** the two boys. He held a wallet in his hand, and he showed it to Danny. "Is this your wallet?"

he asked Danny. "I think I saw you drop it on the floor."

"Yes, it's mine! Thanks so much!" said Danny, touched by his kindness and **embarrassed** that for a moment he had been **suspicious** about the boy's intentions.

"I guess I was wrong," said Alex after the boy left.

"Totally!" said Danny. "If I had to be **suspicious** about anybody, it would be Lucy," he added.

"I thought about her, too, but did you see how many chocolate eggs she had when we met her in the woods? Could she have found all those clues and, at the same time, run back to camp and leave a 'generous' gift by our door? It's just impossible," continued Alex.

"I guess you're right," said Danny. "But I'm still **intrigued** about how she found all those eggs. She must be a very lucky girl!"

"Wait, are you **suggesting** that she watched me in the forest scooping the sheep poop, collected the rest of it, ran back to camp, left it by our door and somehow returned to the forest with a handful of chocolate eggs? Where would she find chocolate here, in the middle of nowhere? There's not even a store nearby."

"Yeah, I guess my **hypothesis** is not that solid," admitted Danny. "I'll stop being **suspicious** about Lucy. Actually, let's not talk about this anymore."

"I agree," said Alex. "From this moment, I'm going to stop talking about everything that happened this morning."

The two boys grabbed their food and sat at a table without saying a word. They **ingested** their food without saying a word. They left the table without saying a word. They promised they would stop talking about the morning's events, and that's **precisely** what they did. However, all they could think about was the mysterious prankster.

CHAPTER 20

A **Delicious Contest**

After lunch, all the children headed back into the forest **adjacent** to the camp. They split into two teams for the worm-eating **contest.** The activity required one **contestant** from each team to be blindfolded, spun around three times and guided to eat as many gummy worms as they could in ten minutes. The gummy worms were hanging on tree branches, and the blindfolded **contestants** had to find them by following the spoken directions of their teammates.

Danny was the first **contestant** to represent his team. At first, the spinning made him run around in circles, which the other kids found **hilarious**. But soon he hit upon the right direction and started to **deplete** the tree branches of gummy worms. His mouth was like a vacuum cleaner – one by one, the gummy worms were slurped up without mercy. Then, they were **ferociously** chewed into small pieces and **eventually** sent into the stomach. None of them survived. It was a bad day to be a gummy worm!

After Danny's successful **endeavor**, the kids moved to other **sections** of the forest where more gummy worms were waiting to be **ingested**. One by one, Danny's teammates participated in the **contest,** but no one was as **effective** as he was. The **contestants** from the other team recovered slowly but surely from their defeat.

It was getting late in the afternoon and the score was tight. The kids moved to the last **section** of forest, which was close to the river. It was now Alex's turn to participate in the **contest**.

Alex spun around three times and, with his mouth wide open and his eyes covered with the blindfold, **hurtled** towards the gummy worms. Or at least, he thought he was heading towards the gummy worms. He heard his teammates yelling but could not understand what they were saying due to the noisy river nearby. Surely, they were cheering for him. *Hey, I'm finally becoming popular*, Alex thought. *But where are the worms? My* **appetite** *is increasing by the minute.* **Eventually**, his mouth caught onto something, but it didn't taste like a gummy worm. It tasted like...dirty clothes! And it had a strong smell of onion and ... sheep? Alex lowered his blindfold.

The **solitary** shepherd was standing in front of him with the sleeve of his coat in Alex's mouth. He looked **intrigued**.

"Young man, around here we eat food when we are hungry. You should have told me they aren't feeding you. Here, take this!" The shepherd handed Alex a greasy chunk of pork skin. "You're lucky," he continued. "It was hard this morning when I started to chew it, but now it's much softer."

Alex **succeeded** at smiling politely, **effectively** hiding his **disgust**. He thanked the shepherd for his generous offer, apologized for **deteriorating** his coat, and **rushed** back to his team. He did *not* need another **embarrassing** moment.

The **contest** resumed. This time, Alex promised that he would pay very close attention to what his teammates were telling him. And he did. He found his way to the gummy worms very **effectively**. Guided by his teammates, Alex caught his first **delicious** gummy worm. Yes, it tasted much better than the shepherd's coat! He continued to **effectively** find and eat the worms much faster than the **contestant** representing the other team. It looked like his team was winning. Everything was going very well until... until it wasn't.

CHAPTER 21

The **Hive**

Honeybees are **fascinating** insects. They are famous for working very hard to produce honey. **Typically**, they are not dangerous to humans, but they do attack when they feel threatened. Bees are not **solitary**. They live in **hives**. There are thousands of bees in a **hive**. The **hives** can be man-made and built on the ground, but wild honeybees build their **hives** in high places, such as trees. These **hives** are **typically** hidden inside of the tree, but sometimes they are **exposed**, hanging from the branches.

In the forest **adjacent** to Daris Camp, there was a tree with an **enormous**, **exposed hive** hanging from one of its branches. Apparently, it was well hidden by the leaves, because the counselor who had hung the gummy worm from that branch had not seen it. The counselor was completely **oblivious** to what might happen if someone very **determined** to win the **contest** pulled the gummy worm's string **ferociously**. Someone like Alex.

Sure enough, when Alex **approached** the gummy worm **attached** to that branch, he pulled it hard and **swiftly**. The **hive detached** from the branch and fell right onto Alex's head, then onto the ground. Alex was **intrigued**. What could possibly have hit him in the head? If the prankster was playing tricks on him again, he (or she?) was going too far! Hitting blindfolded people in the head like that was just cruel. As soon as he lowered his blindfold, his eyes grew wide with terror. The **dreadful** reality of his situation was much more **unsettling** than a simple hit in the head.

The **hive** had split in half when it reached the ground, releasing thousands of bees into the air. At first, they were confused, which gave Alex a few seconds to understand what had just happened. But soon, the bees started to look for their **hostile** aggressor. They were **eager** for revenge, and Alex's **anguished** face was the perfect target.

Alex **shrieked** and ran towards his teammates. They were **baffled**. They were too far away to have seen what happened. They grew even more **baffled** as Alex ran right past them and headed towards the river. They tried to ask him what was happening, but he **grumbled** something **unintelligible** as he kept running.

Moments later, the kids noticed a cloud forming above their heads and heard an **unsettling** buzzing noise. It did not take them a long time to understand that the sound was bad news.

"Run!" screamed one of the counselors, and everybody started to run **chaotically**, following Alex towards the river.

CHAPTER 22

The Chase

The **solitary** shepherd was watching his sheep from a distance. The **soothing** sound of the river and the greasy pork skin that he had had for dinner made him sleepy. *Today was a very good day*, he thought. *Quite **entertaining**!* He **smirked** remembering the **hilarious** kids that he had met that day. *I wonder how long these kids will last living in a **rural** area,* he thought to himself. *They take baths in a **frigid** river, they **gargle** with that **disgusting** water, nobody feeds them...*

Just as he was thinking about the kids, he saw Alex coming out of the woods. Running desperately. Again! Then, throwing himself into the river. Again! But this time he merely mingled with the sheep instead of drinking the water.

What's wrong with this kid? the shepherd thought. He felt the **urge** to tell him that his sheep had fleas, and rubbing against them might not be a good idea, but why ruin the fun? His **smirk** was now **devious**. Why **urge** the boy to stay away from the sheep when he could instead watch him starting to scratch and scratch and scratch? The shepherd decided to sit back and enjoy the show. But what happened next took him completely by surprise.

A large group of kids came out of the woods yelling. Just like Alex had. They jumped into the river. Just like Alex had. And they **approached** the sheep. Just like Alex had. Now, this was **intriguing**. *Who are these kids and what do they want?* wondered the shepherd.

Suddenly, an **unsettling** thought came to his mind. The kids were not there to take baths together with his flea-**infested** sheep! If everybody was as hungry as Alex was, there could be only one reason why they were there. To eat his sheep!

The shepherd's **smirk** disappeared. He remembered how Alex had bit into his coat and he now had no doubt that the boy would eat anything. He became **enraged**. **Detaching** a thick branch from the nearest tree, he **approached** the kids.

"Shoo, shoo! You hungry barbarians! Don't you dare try to eat my sheep!" the shepherd yelled, waiving the branch in the air. He was now **certain** that Alex had only pretended to not be hungry when he refused the **delicious** pork skin. Clearly, he had only wanted to get reinforcements and try for bigger pieces of meat. His sheep, to be more **precise**. What a **devious** kid! You couldn't trust anybody these days!

"Away from my sheep you beasts!" he kept yelling at the kids.

Danny was near Alex when he heard the shepherd.

"I think our friend is **urging** us to leave his sheep alone," Danny told Alex.

"But who isn't leaving them alone?" asked Alex **intrigued**. "We are only trying to get away from the bees."

"I know that, you know that ... I think even the sheep know that. But our friend looks very serious with that stick in his hand. Can we explain what happened to a **suspicious enraged** man?"

The two boys looked at each other. They assessed the danger and yelled to everybody, "This guy is chasing us! Run for your lives!" When the other kids saw the **hostile** look on the shepherd's face, they did not need any more warnings. They took off immediately.

By the time the shepherd got to his sheep, there was no kid nearby. They had all disappeared into the woods, out of sight.

CHAPTER 23

Inconvenience

The kids returned to camp safely. As soon as they **arrived**, they told the counselors all the details about how they had miraculously escaped the bees, and how an angry shepherd had chased them. Christina and another counselor, Andreea, left immediately to look for the shepherd, hoping to clarify the misunderstanding. They found him by the river. The counselors apologized for the **inconvenience** created by the children.

"**Inconvenience**?" asked the shepherd. "That was no **inconvenience**," he explained. The counselors were **relieved** to hear that. What a nice guy! Then, the shepherd continued.

"**Inconvenience** is when you prepare yourself a wrapped sausage for lunch and you find out later that there is no sausage in the wrappings because your dog has eaten it. Or when a nasty fly **accidentally** drowns in your cup of milk. That's **inconvenience**. What happened earlier was a **deliberate** attack! Those unfed creatures would have eaten my sheep on the spot if I had not been there to protect them. My poor babies!"

The counselors explained to the shepherd that the kids had been running away from bees.

"I understand now," the shepherd said. The counselors were **relieved** that the shepherd seemed to be reasonable.

"So, you're telling me that those hungry beasts tried to eat the honey from the **hive**, but when the bees attacked them, they got scared, ran away and decided to eat my sheep instead? My poor little fluffy babies?"

"Oh no, sir," Cristina tried to clarify the confusion. "These kids do not eat raw animals!"

"Animals?" asked the shepherd, **intrigued**.

"Uh, I mean... lovely, fluffy, little cuties like your sheep. Look at them, how sweet they are!"

"Sweet?" The shepherd was becoming **enraged**. Christina was **exasperated**. Was there anything she could say without hurting his feelings?

"She meant that your sheep look very beautiful," Andreea explained. "No, we do not think your sheep are sweet! We don't know how the sheep taste because we don't eat sheep. But they are truly beautiful! Look at this one, how gracefully she's licking your fingers!"

"Ma'am, that is my dog. But he is beautiful, too, isn't he?"

Andreea looked at the muddy dog, now drooling on the shepherd's shoes.

"He's a beauty! Magnificent! You are a truly fortunate man to have such an **elegant** and handsome friend!" she said quickly. Her **compliments** were far from the truth, but they **succeeded** at **easing** the man's **anxiety**. The shepherd listened to what the counselors had to say and **eventually** understood that what he had seen earlier was not a **deliberate** attack on his poor little flea-**infested** cuties.

CHAPTER 24

Lucky

Danny and Alex went to bed early that evening. The **anxiety** of being chased by first the bees and then, the shepherd, had **exhausted** them. In fact, they were just as **exhausted** as they had been the day before, following their rafting **endeavor!**

"Can you believe that the shepherd thought we wanted to eat his **precious** sheep?" asked Alex, fluffing up his pillow to find the perfect sleeping position. He and Danny giggled.

"Well, in his **defense,** can you imagine how **terrifying** a group of kids might look when they come out of the woods running **chaotically** towards the river?" asked Danny.

"Not as **terrifying** as a cloud of **enraged** wild bees protecting their **precious hive**!" said Alex. "I think I will have **nightmares** tonight! So if I kick you in my sleep, in my **defense**, I have a good reason for it," he continued with a **smirk**.

"Oh sure, no problem! Do that and I'll tie you to the bed. *In my defense*," replied Danny, playing along.

"Seriously, dude. That was **terrifying**! When I lowered my blindfold and saw all those bees coming out of the **hive**, I thought they would cover me in honey and then mummify me!"

"Yes, that was **dreadful**! We're lucky nobody got stung!" said Danny scratching his head. "Today could have ended much worse! Thank goodness nobody was harmed."

"I totally **agree** with you," said Alex scratching his feet. "We are very lucky! The fact that nobody was harmed is a miracle," he added, as he slowly fell asleep.

"It is… a miracle…", mumbled Danny, falling asleep himself. "We are… lucky…"

As they slept, the boys continued to scratch their heads, their necks, their arms, and their feet. And so did every other kid in the camp.

CHAPTER 25

Flea **Infestation**

Fleas are very small insects. They are **parasites**. That means that they need a **host** in order to survive. The **host** can be a mammal, a bird, or a human. Fleas feed off their **hosts** by biting their skin and drinking their blood. Fleabites **typically** look like small red bumps on the skin. The bites are usually not dangerous to humans, but if you scratch the bumps, they will get bigger, and the itch will worsen.

People can get fleas from animals. When people get too close to a flea-**infested** animal (such as a sheep), the fleas can change **hosts** by jumping onto the people and hiding in their hair or underneath their clothes. Then, they start biting and sucking their blood. Fleabites may go **unnoticed** in the beginning because they are very tiny. However, if they are not treated immediately and people continue to scratch them, the itching increases and the bites are more likely to be **noticed**.

On Wednesday morning, the kids from Daris Camp learned that they were not so lucky after all. Or at least, not as lucky as they thought they were. They learned it the hard way.

"Baby vampires!!!" a loud **shriek** came from cabin eight. It was Alex, who, upon waking and looking in the mirror, saw many tiny bites on his neck.

Danny jumped out of bed and looked at Alex, and then, in the mirror. He was even more **disturbed** than Alex, because he had small bites all over his face. He tried to wipe the red spots away, hoping it was just another strawberry jam prank. But this time, the red dots did not go away.

"AAAHHHHHH!" Danny ran out of the cabin, screaming and waking everybody up. "Baby vampires! We were attacked by baby vampires!"

The kids from the camp came out of their cabins to see what was going on. They were still wearing their pajamas. To Danny's surprise, everybody else had the same reaction. Their necks and their faces were covered with tiny dots. They looked at each other, **horrified**, and pointed out one another's bite marks. They were **certain** that baby vampires had attacked them during the night. Obviously, it was a whole nursery of baby vampires, not just a few. What else could it be? Some kids developed the story and imagined that the victims of the vampires would turn into vampires themselves and grow fangs. But would that be true even if you are bitten by a baby vampire? The kids started to check one another's mouths, looking for fangs. The whole scene resembled a group visit to the dentist. In pajamas.

Danny **approached** Lucy. He said, "Take a look in my mouth, Lucy! Do you see anything **abnormal**?" He opened his mouth wide.

"If your yellow teeth and that nasty cavity seem normal to you, then no, I don't see anything **abnormal**," she replied. Danny's teeth were not yellow, and he did not have any cavities, but Lucy could not help taking advantage of a **gullible**, scared child. "Oh, wait a minute, I see something!" she continued.

"You do? You do?!" cried Danny, **horrified** by the thought that she had spotted a fang growing in his mouth.

"Yes, I do. Let me take a closer look." Lucy stuck two fingers deep inside Danny's mouth and got nearer him. "I think you have some steak leftovers between your teeth. But phew! Your breath stinks! You know, these days we have this thing called toothpaste. You should try it sometime, my friend."

Danny was just about to explain to Miss **Compliment** that the last thing he needed was one of her **sarcastic** remarks – and yes, he was using toothpaste every morning (when he was not bitten by baby vampires), when the mouth-checking pajama party was interrupted by the camp counselors. They took one look at the kids and immediately called for the nurse.

An hour later, the mystery had been solved. Apparently, all the kids who had tried to escape the bee attack by jumping into the shallow river had mingled with the flea-**infested** sheep and returned to camp with **parasites** all over them. They had been completely **oblivious** about what they were bringing back to the camp! These kids generously and unintentionally shared the fleas with all of their friends, and it did not take long before the whole camp was **infested**. During the night, the kids started to scratch in their sleep, so the fleabites became more visible. The tiny dots on their skin might have looked like baby vampire bites in the morning, but they were nothing but fleabites. A gift from those poor little fluffy cuties.

CHAPTER 26

A **Devious** Plan

The flea infestation wreaked **havoc** on Daris Camp. The kids formed a long line in front of the nurse's office. A long, *scratchy* line, to be more **precise**. The kids looked **hilarious**. They knew that the more they scratched, the worse it would itch, but some of them just could not help it and kept on scratching. Baby vampire bites? Forget that! Soon, some kids would look like they had been bitten by teen vampires.

Danny and Alex were waiting their turn to be seen by the nurse. With great **stoicism**, they resisted the **urge** to scratch.

"Can you believe that such a tiny insect could wreak such **havoc**?" asked Alex. "The counselors had to call in professionals to take care of every cabin and all of our belongings!"

"That's a **relief!** It would be **horrifying** to think that we would have to deal with the fleabites for one more night," said Danny. "What **intrigues** me the most is: how can the shepherd be **immune** to the fleas? He lives among his **precious** sheep, but he doesn't seem to be bothered by fleabites."

"Fleabites?" Alex remembered the shepherd's strong onion **odor**. "He smells so bad that I'm sure he needs to beg the fleas to bite him. Maybe even blackmail them - *Hey, if none of you will bite me today, I will shear my sheep bald!* I'm sure he's **immune** to fleabites because his blood is poisonous to any **parasite**. If the fleas had a constitution, the first article would say: *Stay away from smelly shepherds.*"

"And the second article would say: *Alex is good for you. Bite him with no mercy and **deplete** him of his **delicious** blood*," continued Danny.

"I'm sure that article would have an amendment," clarified Alex. "It would say: *By the way, don't forget to jump on Danny, too.*" The boys giggled.

"Hey, maybe a strong **odor** is truly a good **defense** mechanism against bites!" said Danny. "It's **inconvenient** because it drives people away, but at least it makes you **immune** to insects!"

"It's not that **inconvenient** if you **deliberately** choose a **solitary** way of life," explained Alex. "Or if the people around you are as stinky as you are!"

Danny thought for a while at what Alex just said. Then he asked his friend, "Hey, what if the onion **odor** really would make our blood **disgusting** and **immune** to any bites? You know, fleas? Vampires?"

Alex started to like where this conversation was going.

"Are you saying that we should start eating lots of onions?" he asked Danny with a **smirk**.

"Why not? If we both do it, we'll be **immune** to each other's smells, and we'll keep away the **parasites** and other threats. What do you think of this plan?" asked Danny.

"It's **devious**, but I LOVE it! Let's do it!"

CHAPTER 27

Repellent

The morning went by very quickly. Between the mouth-checking pajama party, a quick breakfast, nurse visits, and getting the cabins treated for fleas, everybody in the camp was busily getting ready to get their life back to normal. So busily that they did not **notice** Danny and Alex sneaking in and out of the kitchen with their hands and pockets full of onions. Nobody **noticed** the two kids gulping down onion after onion until their eyes started watering and their faces turned red and sweaty. Nobody **noticed** anything... until lunch time.

Danny and Alex had just grabbed their lunches and sat down at their table when Lucy **approached** them.

"Hey guys, guess what... Whoa! What's wrong with you tomato-heads? Are you sick?"

"What are you talking about?" asked Danny pretending he had no idea what she meant.

"WHAT AM I TALKING ABOUT?!" Lucy yelled. Her reaction was anything but **discreet**. Now everybody in the cafeteria had stopped eating and was looking at them. "What am I talking about? You look like two bottles of ketchup with clothes on, and you don't find anything **abnormal** about that? Your eyes are drowning in a pool of tears – they are practically begging for a life jacket - , and you are telling me, *Nah, there's nothing wrong! My eyeballs love swimming like that.*"

Alex knew he needed to come up with a good excuse if he didn't want to **expose** their plan. He told Lucy, "The truth is, we miss home! Can you tell that we've been crying?" Then he squeezed out a fake sob.

Lucy felt a sudden **urge** to comfort the two boys.

"Oh, I'm so sorry! Let me give you a hug..." She gave Alex a huge hug. For a whole second. Then she **swiftly** backed away holding her nose. "Wow! What did they put in your food? You smell awful! Danny, stay away from that plate!" She stepped toward Danny, trying to save him from what she believed was **infested** food, then backed away again, even more **horrified**. She looked like she was about to **faint**!

"Eew, dude! Did anybody switch your deodorant with an insect **repellent** spray? You smell worse than you did in the morning! Are you **decomposing**?"

"Yes Lucy, I'm a zombie. Did you just notice that?" replied Danny **sarcastically**.

"Seriously guys, that awful **odor** of yours could **repel** any living creature on Earth!" said Lucy, and she immediately walked away.

The other kids from the lunchroom who had witnessed the scene also decided to stay away from the two boys. They all crammed in together at other tables or found a place on the floor. None of them wanted to take any chances of being **infested** with a virus. Plus, the **odor** coming from the two boys was **pervasive** and **repellent**.

Danny and Alex smiled at each other. Their plan seemed to work. At least with the humans.

CHAPTER 28

Too Easy!

A ropes course is an exciting but challenging outdoor activity. The participants in this activity are expected to go through a **network** of **stations** connected to one another. They are expected to pass from **station** to **station** until they

reach the last one. Some **sections** of a rope course are more challenging than others, but a **typical** ropes course starts out quite easy, with its difficulty increasing at each station.

Many ropes courses are built in the woods, and some of the **stations** are actually built into the tree trunks. These **stations** are connected by thick wire cables, ropes, and wooded walkways. Although the ropes courses do not seem **terrifying** when seen from the ground level, some participants get scared once they reach the top. However, if they follow the directions and safety procedures, there is nothing to worry about.

Soon after lunch, the children from Daris Camp were scheduled to participate in one such ropes course challenge. They all met Dorin in the forest **adjacent** to the camp where an **enormous network** of **stations** was waiting to be conquered. The kids couldn't see the entire **network**, but the first **sections** looked fun and **fascinating**!

Dorin gathered the kids around him. "Listen to me, boys and girls! Today is a great day! A day that you will remember for the rest of your lives!"

"What?" yelled Lucy **abruptly**. "I can't believe it! Is it really happening? Danny! Alex! Your parents are here to take your stinky, **decomposing**, *'precious'* selves back home! We can finally breathe fresh air! This is the best day ever!"

"No, Lucy! Nobody is leaving!" Dorin stopped her **abruptly** before she could continue her **devious** plan to **deliberately** put down the two boys because of their **repellent** onion **odor**. But the boys were **immune** to her mean comments. They were too busy trying to chase away a group of flies that were attracted by their **odor**; it had been bothering them since they first **arrived** in the woods. The boys completely ignored Lucy's new *'compliments'*.

Dorin continued. "Today is the day when some of you will conquer one of the greatest **anxieties** known to humans: the fear of heights! As you move between the **stations** of this **network**, it is very important to follow the directions I will give you. I **urge** you to take this very seriously, because I don't want anybody to get **injured**." Then, Dorin started to give everyone **adequate** training on how to navigate the **network**.

Danny and Alex looked at the first **section**. It was just a log sitting on the ground. Above it, stretched a wire cable that was supposed to help the participants keep their balance.

"Fear of heights?" whispered Danny. "What is Dorin talking about? That doesn't look **terrifying** at all! How could anybody get **injured** falling off a log, anyway?"

"That's exactly what I was thinking!" replied Alex, trying with both hands to repel the flies that were bothering them. "And did you see the second **section**? Who would fall off that rope balance bridge? Its sides are as high as our shoulders."

"Yes, and look at the third **section**, up in the tree!" agreed Danny. "It's basically a long wooden barrel with both ends open. All you have to do is crawl from one **station** to another and hang on to that wire cable above your head! A baby could do this with his eyes closed!"

"This is too easy!" **agreed** Alex.

After describing the ropes **network**, Dorin equipped each child with a **harness**. He explained to the participants how to **properly** secure themselves by **attaching** the **harness** to the cable above their heads with a strong metal loop called a **carabiner**. He insisted that this **attachment** was mandatory, and its purpose was to protect the children from any **unpleasant events**. He **urged** the children to take some time and practice handling the **carabiner properly**.

Danny and Alex were **relieved** when the training was over. So boring! Who needed all that safety training anyway? The two boys were ready to start climbing! It's no wonder they were **grateful** when the other kids chose them to go first! How nice of them! Of course, at that point, every kid in the camp would do anything to keep the two boys' onion **odor** as far away from them as possible.

CHAPTER 29

The Ropes Course

Danny was the first to start the ropes course challenge, hopping onto the log. Alex immediately followed. And so did the group of flies that had been bothering them ever since they had entered the forest.

"Hey, look at me, I'm the Log Rider!" Danny said to Alex, acting like he was riding a surfboard. "I'm the Master of the Logs!" he continued, **boasting** about his ability to keep his balance.

"Ooh, watch out, my friend! You might fall and get a boo-boo," Alex replied **sarcastically**, making sure that nobody but Danny could hear him. Then, continuing to **mock** Dorin he said, "I **urge** you to take this challenge seriously, so you don't get **injured**. Did you **attach** your **harness properly** to the wire? Did you check your **carabiner**?"

The two boys giggled as they moved to the second **station**. Alex could not wait until Danny passed through the rope bridge and jumped on right behind him. Crossing the bridge made them feel like two explorers in the jungle! The bridge moved unexpectedly up and down and back and forth, but it was strong enough to hold the two boys. They were bouncing up and down and left and right with every step they took. It was really fun! It was so exciting, they were **oblivious** to the fact that the group of flies buzzing around them was growing larger.

Next, the boys climbed a rope ladder to reach the third **station** up in a tree. From there, they both **hurtled** inside the long barrel at the same time. They started crawling through the barrel, but as soon as they reached its middle **section**, the barrel started swinging, too, just as the rope bridge had. Only this time, neither of the boys was laughing. Danny and Alex looked through the cracks of the barrel and realized they were very far from the ground. If the ropes broke, they would take a nasty fall. If that **section** had a name, it would have been *The Silent Barrel*. Nobody was **boasting** anymore. Nobody was **mocking** anyone. The boys started to **shiver** with fear.

"Go, Danny! Move! Come on, let's get out of here before the barrel swings any faster!" Alex **urged** his friend, pushing him towards the exit. The boys crawled to the other end of the moving barrel and **eventually** managed to reach the next **station**.

"Phew! That one was pretty **unsettling**," said Danny. "I wonder what comes next."

In the next **section**, the boys had to move between **stations** by walking along a series of logs. Danny went first, but as soon as he stepped with both feet on the first log, it began swinging back and forth. Danny held onto the cable above his head with both hands. The look on his face was not **settling**.

"Hey, wait for me! I can't do this all by myself!" said Alex, as he stepped onto the log with one foot. For a second, the log stopped moving.

"Alex, don't forget to **attach** your **carabiner** to the cable!" Danny tried to warn his friend. But it was too late. Alex had already stepped his second foot onto the log, and now the log was swinging even faster. Alex grabbed Danny from behind, one arm around his friend's throat and the other one around his waist.

"Danny, this is **terrifying**!"

"Really?" asked Danny with **stoicism**, although he felt the same way. He was grasping tightly to the wire while trying hard to keep his balance and, at the same time, loosen Alex's grip on his throat. "Then why didn't you **attach** your **carabiner** to the wire?"

"I forgot all about that! I didn't want you to leave without me! I wanted us to work together! As a team! I wanted us to work **effectively**!" explained Alex.

"**Fabulous**!" said Danny **sarcastically**. "Then, here's a tip for **effective** teamwork: Stop choking your partner! Loosen your grip and let me breathe **properly**. Another tip? Grab the **carabiner** and **attach** it to the wire!"

"I wish I could but I ... I don't want to let you go! This is **dreadful**!" wailed Alex.

"OK, then, let me do it for you!" Danny turned and tried to grab the **carabiner**, but Alex held him even tighter.

"Please wait until the log stops moving," said Alex, and he closed his eyes, pretending it was all just a **nightmare**. He was hoping that when he opened his eyes, everything would be just fine.

Chapter 30

The **Triple** Hug

The log **eventually** stopped moving, but when Alex opened his eyes, everything was not fine. In fact, a **nightmare** would have been better than the **events** that were about to follow. Here's what happened...

First, Alex **noticed** the group of flies buzzing around them. "Hey, Danny, did you **notice** that the flies buzzing around us are now more **numerous** than they were earlier? I think they brought their entire family here."

"I think they brought their family AND their whole neighborhood," said Danny. "And they are not just

numerous. Look how hungry they are! They think they came to a block party. They're looking at me like I'm a hot dog."

"Yeah, I feel like I have my own **satellites orbiting** around my head," agreed Alex.

"I wish they would choose a different **orbit**," said Danny trying to **repel** them. He could not take his hand off the wire, so he was trying to puff them away with his breath. "Alex, I think one of your **satellites** is trying to get in my nose. If I take my hand off the wire, we might fall. So, I won't. But please slap this fly on my behalf."

"I would gladly do that, but I'm afraid to let you go! I might fall!" said Alex.

"Dude, if I fall, we BOTH fall! Hurry up and **repel** them! I can feel them nibbling on my earwax! It's tickling me!"

"I can't take my hands off you! Just look down – it's **horrifying**!" yelled Alex, squeezing Danny even harder.

Just as the two boys began hugging each other even more tightly, a second unexpected thing happened. They heard Lucy's voice behind them.

"Hey, look at these guys! Aren't you the cutest and sweetest friends ever? You must have missed each other so badly! Hey, boys, do you feel the need of a **triple** hug?" For a moment, she completely forgot about their smell.

"No!" yelled the boys.

"Come on, don't be shy!" said Lucy as she stepped onto the log. Of course, the log started to swing again. This move took Lucy by surprise. She **swiftly** reached out and grabbed Alex tightly. Now, the **triple** hug was truly complete.

"Danny, I now have another **satellite** around me," said Alex with **stoicism**. "This one is much bigger than the others. What should

I do?"

"Just open your mouth and keep talking," said Danny. "The onion **odor** will soon convince her to change **orbit.**"

"I don't think she can do that. She forgot to **attach** her **carabiner**."

"Oops! I guess a **triple** hug was not the best idea," admitted Lucy. She had just realized that the only kid on that swinging log whose **harness** was **properly attached** to the wire was Danny. Would his **harness** be strong enough to hold everybody if one of them began to fall? Or would the **triple** hug become a **triple** fall? Luckily, nobody moved. *Nothing to worry about*, thought Lucy. *We'll just wait until the log stops swinging, and then we'll slowly figure out how to walk safely to the next* **station**. *Easy-peasy.*

Unfortunately, her plan did not quite work out, because the next **event** took everybody by surprise once more. A squirrel who was walking on the branch above the kids lost its balance and dropped the walnut it was carrying. The nut hit Danny on the head and rolled under his shirt. The squirrel followed the nut. Before Danny could say anything, the squirrel was completely under his shirt!

CHAPTER 31

The **Fortunate** Kids

The flies nibbling on Danny's earwax were not his biggest problem anymore. He had a bigger one under his clothes. A scratchy problem with a furry tail.

The squirrel found the walnut and ran **chaotically** around Danny's waist trying to find a way out from under his shirt. It wreaked **havoc** among the three kids. Danny panicked. He took his hands off the wire and tried to pull his shirt off, to let the squirrel go. At first, he could not do that because Alex was still holding his waist

very tightly. Danny pushed Alex's hands off him, and **eventually** managed to pull his shirt out of his pants. The squirrel shot out from under his shirt like a rocket. Danny was **fortunate**.

Alex was less **fortunate**. Not having Danny to hang on to, and with Lucy pushing tightly against him, Alex lost his balance. He fell off the swinging log, dragging Lucy with him. As he was going down, Alex tried to reach the wire above him, but he missed it. Instead, he grabbed Danny's left shoe. That stopped their fall. For two seconds. That's how long it took Danny's shoe to come off of his foot. After that, Alex continued his fall with Lucy wrapped around him like the colorful paper on a Christmas present. She was one faithful **satellite**! All the other **satellites** had buzzed away in the confusion.

Alex and Lucy were **horrified**. With their eyes squeezed shut, they screamed their lungs out waiting for the **unfortunate** moment of their crash. But the crash didn't happen. They were **fortunate** this time. Alex's hood got caught in a tree branch and their fall was stopped once again. But how long would it last this time? Would it be more than two seconds? The boy and girl continued screaming without daring to open their eyes. Then, they heard a familiar voice talking to them.

"Lucy, I'm so glad that Alex's **odor** does not bother you anymore!" It was Dorin. What was he doing up in the air? Had he grown wings?

"You can let go of him now," the counselor **urged** the girl. *What is he talking about? Does he **deliberately** want to make me fall?* thought Lucy. *What's wrong with him?*

"Both of you can stop screaming," Dorin continued **undisturbed**.

The two **terrified** kids opened their eyes. Dorin was standing in front of them. Standing, not flying. The kids looked down. Their screams faded into a muffled squeaking noise. They could see that their feet were almost touching the ground. Yes, the branch that

Alex's hood was hooked onto was THAT close to the ground. **Fortunately**.

Dorin unwrapped Lucy from around Alex and lowered her to the ground. Then, he unhooked Alex from the branch. The kids were finally safe now. Nobody was **injured**. What a scare! They themselves promised they would always follow the instructions from then on. Especially those that required the use of a **carabiner** and a **harness**. Alex also promised himself to never **mock** a counselor again. And Lucy promised herself to never rely on Alex again. The kids continued to make **numerous** silent promises until their thoughts were interrupted by a voice coming from above.

"Uh, guys, can I have my shoe back?"

CHAPTER 32

The **Feast**

Lucy and Alex had learned their lesson. The rest of the afternoon went smoothly, and the ropes course challenge was completed without any other **unfortunate events**. Every kid in the camp had a blast! Yes, it was **terrifying** at times. Yes, they often wished they had never agreed to do it. But in the end, their **dread** was replaced with **satisfaction**. They returned to the camp that evening with a great feeling of pride: they had tested their limits and conquered their fears. They also returned with **numerous** adventures to **boast** about.

When the kids **arrived** at the camp, there was an **enormous** surprise awaiting them! A **delicious**, mouth-watering surprise, to be more **precise**. The counselors had decided that the best way to **appease** the children after their **dreadful** flea **infestation** experience was to transform their normal dinner into a **feast**. And what a **feast** it was!

The moment they entered the cafeteria, the children were welcomed by an open pasta bar. That's right! They could eat as much pasta as their stomach could hold. **Unfortunately**, they only had one stomach each! The children had such a hard time choosing between the yummy-looking fettuccini served with parmesan cheese sauce and the mile-long spaghetti topped with **enormous** meatballs drowned in marinara sauce. To make the decision even harder, a few steps away from the pasta bar was a variety of pizzas topped with perfectly melted cheese waiting to be **ingested** in a heartbeat. For those who did not like pizzas or pastas (strange as that may be!), there was another table covered with plates of crispy French fries with gigantic hotdogs and hamburgers with a **triple** layer of patties. Next, there were apple pies and raspberry pies topped with melted vanilla ice cream. There was fruit, too! The children had a hard time choosing between the fresh golden apples, the juicy grapes, the **delicious**-looking pineapple, and the plump peaches. But wait! No strawberries? No, the strawberries were not there. They were just a few steps away. On sticks, near the marshmallows, by the… by the chocolate fountain! Yes, they even had their own chocolate fountain where they could dip as many marshmallows and strawberries as they liked! Everything was so **appealing** that it would have been **abnormal** to be **immune** to such a sight.

Danny and Alex looked at the feast in **disbelief**, and their mouths dropped open.

"This must be the mother of all **feasts**!" gasped Danny completely **fascinated** by the scene before him.

"I have never seen so much food in my life!" whispered Alex. "This is **fabulous**!"

Lucy approached the two boys looking very **intrigued**. "Did I just die and reach food heaven? Hey, Alex, pinch me! Pinch me! Tell me I'm not dreaming!"

Alex pinched Lucy's cheek.

"Ouch! Why did you do that? What's wrong with you?" yelled Lucy.

Alex was **baffled**.

"I'm sorry! You just asked me to do it," said Alex.

"I'm just messing with you my **gullible** friend," replied Lucy with a **satisfied deceitful smirk**. "So, are you going to enjoy this **feast**, or do you prefer the shepherd's half-chewed pork skin?"

"I think I'm going to go ask him to keep it for you, just in case you run out of tasty jokes!" replied Alex, **embarrassed** that he had let her **deceive** him again.

Danny decided to step in and end the conversation **abruptly**.

"Guys, there's a **feast** waiting for us! You'd better stop this nonsense and grab a plate!"

Lucy admitted that her jokes were not quite **elegant**, and she apologized for her behavior. Then, she grabbed a plate and got in line. Alex got in line, too, but he decided that one plate was not enough to completely **satisfy** his **appetite**. So, he grabbed three instead!

CHAPTER 33

Full

After the **feast**, Danny and Alex headed back to their cabin, dragging their feet. It was late in the evening.

"I'm so stuffed, I think I'm going to explode!" exclaimed Danny.

"Tell me about it!" agreed Alex. "My stomach **expanded** so much that I look like I just swallowed a soccer ball! Who knew that the stomach could be so **flexible**?"

"It's crazy, right? Just imagine: when your stomach is empty, it can be as small as an egg, but when you eat a lot, it can **expand** to many times its size," explained Danny.

"I wish I could be as **flexible** as my stomach! When I played basketball, I would stretch all the way up to the hoop!"

"Or you could **expand** your butt to block every player on the court," added Danny with a chuckle.

"I just hope tomorrow morning they'll let us sleep in as long as we want, so our stomachs can have enough time to break down the food we just ate. We deserve a break!" continued Alex.

"I don't think the counselors have that kind of **flexibility**. Don't you know that tomorrow we're scheduled to go on the cave exploration? The cave is far from here. We'll need to get up early in the morning!"

"Oh, man! Do we really have to?"

"I'm afraid so," said Danny empathetically. "We'd better get to bed as soon as possible."

The two friends reached their cabin, fell onto their beds, and fell asleep **instantaneously**. They were **depleted** of all energy. After another day full of **events** including keeping their balance on swinging-logs, both of the kids slept like logs themselves.

CHAPTER 34

Thursday

The kids from Daris Camp woke up early the next morning, just as Danny had **predicted**. They prepared for a long two-hour hike to a **remote** location in the heart of the mountains.

"Hey boys, did you hear that the cave we're going to visit is actually an ice cave?" Lucy greeted the two boys from cabin number eight.

"What do you mean? Do they sell ice cream inside the cave?" asked Alex.

"No, the cave **literally** has ice in it. I know it sounds crazy, because it's summer and we've been wearing shorts and t-shirts all week, but I **suggest** you pack warm jackets, because it's going to get cold inside," explained Lucy. "The ice caves have **numerous** spots of **perennial** ice, which means that the temperature inside the cave will be at or below freezing."

"Per animal ice? What is that? A type of ice-cream flavor for animals?" asked Alex rubbing his tummy. *Hmm, how bad can it be?* he thought.

"No, silly! All you can think about is food! **Perennial** ice means that the ice never melts. It's there year-round."

"How is that possible?" asked Danny. "Does that mean that we're going to go deep underground?"

"Deep and far! You'd better get your flashlights ready!" Lucy **urged** them as she walked away and headed towards the counselors.

"Does she mean that **literally**, or is she trying to **deceive** us again?" Alex asked his friend.

"Well, you know how **devious** Lucy can be at times. You can never trust her. She is a **perennial** joker," said Danny. "My **hypothesis** is that she is trying to **deceive** us again. It's kind of **suspicious** how **eager** she was to **reveal** this news to us. I **assume** the cave can't be *that* cold. It's summer!"

"Yeah. When she said that we were going to eat worms, we took her comment **literally**, and it turned out that she was **deliberately** trying to make us feel **anxious**. She **succeeded** then, but I'm **determined** to not let that happen again. It would be ridiculous to fill our bags with warm clothes. Plus, it's too **inconvenient** to carry a large and heavy flashlight during a two-hour hike, so I'm not going to," concluded Alex.

"I have a tiny flashlight. I think it should be enough for the two of us. We'll just stick to the group and we'll be fine," said Danny.

The boys joined the group **eager** to start another **fabulous** day.

CHAPTER 35

Crowded

The morning hike was **pleasant**. The group **proceeded** hiking enthusiastically towards its destination, taking advantage of the cool, fresh morning air. Soon, the sun would be up and burning **ferociously**. The counselors were right. They *needed* to leave early in the morning to avoid the **hostile** mid-day sun.

"Are we there yet?" Alex soon started whining.

Danny was puzzled.

"Alex, we just left two minutes ago! We have another 118 minutes left in the hike! So no, we're not there just yet!"

"Are you sure it's only been two minutes? It feels more like an **eternity**!" asked Alex in **disbelief**.

"I don't want to sound unempathetic, but you need to pull yourself together, dude! It's going to be a long day!"

"I know that, but I'm having a hard time explaining that to my stomach!" Alex continued whining.

"What do you mean?"

"Don't you hear the **enraged grumbling** sounds coming out from under my shirt?"

"I heard some noises, but I thought they were just some **slimy** frogs greeting us from the river banks," explained Danny.

"Well, unless those **slimy** frogs were fried and added to the layers of hamburgers that we had last night, then no - it wasn't any frog making that noise. It was my stomach. To be more **precise**, it was the grapes that I ate last night. They are arguing with the peaches. They can't seem to **agree** on who **arrived** there first."

"Really? I didn't know that the fruit could be so competitive! Who's winning?" asked Danny.

"I'm not sure. They **arrived** in my stomach as a married couple, but I think they are getting a divorce and one of them is about to leave," explained Alex.

"Are you saying that…"

"Yes, some of the fruits that I ate last night wants to **proceed** towards the exit. They did not like the party. It was not very **entertaining** for them," added Alex.

"No wonder they didn't like your party! Last night you had three full plates!" exclaimed Danny **exasperated**. "Your **expanded** stomach was a very busy place. Who likes being crowded like that?"

"Are you saying that my grapes stepped all over my peaches, and the pasta wrapped around the French fries, which could not dance because their feet stumbled into the **slimy** jelly that I had with the cake? And then when the hamburgers squeezed the mustard out of the hot dogs, which were already crowded by the donuts that I had as an appetizer, everybody got mad and started a fight?"

"Gosh, Alex, is that all you ate?" asked Danny **sarcastically**.

"No, I also had the apple pie topped with vanilla ice-cream, but they **arrived** at the party a little bit later," explained Alex. "They **literally** had to wait in line about ten minutes, because there was no room in the lobby."

"You mean in your mouth, right? I remember you being silent all evening because your cheeks were stuffed, just like a hamster's. Seeing your face plump like that was pretty funny, I have to admit," confessed Danny.

"You have to **agree** that last night's **feast** was **delicious.** But maybe **ingesting** so much food was not a smart move," admitted Alex.

"A mild stomachache is **typical** after such an **enormous** meal," Danny tried to **ease** the **anguish** of his friend. "Maybe it will go away on its own."

"Maybe," replied Alex in **disbelief.** He promised to himself to remain **stoic** and stop whining. Maybe all the fruit in his stomach would stop **disagreeing** with each other and **eventually** get along. Maybe they would **proceed** towards the exit only in the evening, after the kids returned to the camp. Maybe the only **grumbling** sounds they would hear in the near future really would be made by the **slimy** frogs laying on the riverbank.

CHAPTER 36

Barbie Dolls

Finally, the group **arrived** at the cave. **Fortunately**, Alex had not required an **instantaneous** emergency break, and everybody made it there before the sun became too **hostile**. Now, the kids divided into small groups to start making their **descent**.

Danny, Alex, and Lucy were in the last group, led by Christina. Upon entering the cave, they were welcomed by a **pervasive** chill. Everybody took their jackets out of their backpacks and got **suitably** bundled up for the new **environment** that they were about to explore. Everybody, that is, except Danny and Alex.

"Hey boys, where are your jackets?" Lucy asked the two boys. "This is a good time to put them on. The more we **descend**, the colder it will get," she clarified.

"I… hmmm…" **grumbled** Alex **unintelligibly**.

"You know… we… well… funny thing… actually…" Danny didn't **succeed** at being much more **intelligible** than his friend.

"Don't tell me you didn't bring your jackets!" Lucy stopped and stared at them in **disbelief**. "I **literally** told you to do that just this morning!" She looked **exasperated**. "Look at you now, all pale and **shivering**! If anyone touched you, they would get scratched by your goosebumps!"

"Well, it's true that you **suggested**..." Danny tried to find an excuse.

"How old are you, anyway – four?! Should I have told you that you were *required* to bring a jacket with you? What did you expect me to do? MAKE YOU take a jacket with you?! I thought you were old enough to be responsible."

Danny and Alex were **embarrassed**. Today was a bad day to not trust Lucy. Maybe they should start giving her more credit.

"Here," Lucy continued, taking two pink long sleeve shirts out of her backpack. "I packed these extra shirts, but I don't really need them. Put them on, and hopefully your teeth will stop chattering. They are making so much noise, I can't even hear my own thoughts!"

Typical Lucy. But this time, the boys were **immune** to her **sarcastic** comments. They took the shirts and put them on. They didn't care that they were very tight, or even that they didn't **descend** past their belly buttons. They were just happy that the shirts were **flexible** enough that they didn't rip apart when they were put on. The boys also didn't care that the shirts were pink. They didn't care about the unicorns and the **numerous** hearts that covered them. They didn't even care when Lucy gave them another **compliment** by telling them that they looked pretty - just like two Barbie dolls. They were only happy that their teeth were no longer chattering, and everybody could enjoy the silence of the cave.

CHAPTER 37

The Ice Cave

Lucy was right. The more they **descended** into the cave, the colder it felt. The colder it felt, the more **numerous icicles** they saw hanging from the ceiling. Then, just a few minutes after entering the cave, the group **arrived** in a **spectacular** chamber. They all took a break to admire this new **environment**.

"Look at these **stalactites**!" exclaimed Lucy pointing the strong beam of her flashlight to the ceiling.

"Lucy, you're crazy! How can you see any **satellites** inside a cave?" asked Alex.

"I said **stalactites**, not **satellites**! That's the name of these **enormous** mineral deposits hanging from the ceiling of the ice cave, the ones that look like **icicles**."

"Aren't those called **stalagmites**?" asked Danny.

"No. Do you see these deposits that look like they're growing up out of the ground?" asked Lucy.

"Yes, they look exactly the same as the ones that hang down from the ceiling," said Danny.

"That's right. However, the ones coming up from the ground are called **stalagmites**, and the ones hanging down from the ceiling are called **stalactites**," explained Lucy.

"So the ones that look like a stalagmite and a stalactite kissing each other are called stalagmitactites?" asked Danny.

"No, those are called columns because they look like… well, like columns," said Lucy with a **smirk**.

"They look like **enormous** sausages to me," mumbled Alex.

"Of course they do, my dear, famished friend. I'm sure that your **perennial** hunger makes everything you see in this cave look like food," said Lucy.

"Yeah, pretty much," admitted Alex.

"I just wonder how long it took them to grow like that," Danny's train of thoughts continued.

"It **typically** takes about ten years to grow the width of your thumb," answered Lucy.

"You mean the length, right?" asked Danny in **disbelief.**

"No, the width. **Literally**. It's a very slow process. The minerals are carried and deposited by drops of water. If we listen carefully, we might be **fortunate** enough to hear some drops of water falling from the ceiling right now," explained Lucy.

"Really? Let's do that," **suggested** Danny.

Everybody got very quiet. For a few seconds they could not hear anything at all. But just when they thought they were out of luck and they were getting tired of listening, a loud noise **disturbed** the silence. The noise was coming from behind them and it **anguished** every child in the chamber. It sounded like the cave was about to collapse!

CHAPTER 38

Inconvenience

"What was that?" yelled Lucy.

The sound was **horrific**, and its **pervasive** echo **terrified** her. An equally **pervasive** rotten egg smell followed the sound, answering Lucy's question.

"Eew! Alex, is that you?" Danny asked holding his nose.

"Sorry!" Alex felt **relieved** and **embarrassed** at the same time. "I couldn't keep it in any longer! There is a war going on in my stomach."

"Based on the thundering sound you've just made, I'm sure it's going to be **epic**," said Danny. "I bet poets will write **numerous** poems about this day. For years to come, our grandchildren will learn in their history books about the war between the grapes and the peaches that happened on the AES battlefield."

"AES battlefield?" asked Alex **intrigued**.

"Alex's **Expanded** Stomach," clarified Danny.

"Danny, how can you joke about this **dreadful** smell?" **grumbled** Lucy, seriously **disturbed**. "This is not an **epic** poem. If Alex keeps doing this, soon there will be nobody left to write anything. The sounds he makes will cause **stalactites** to crack and crumble. The smell will **suffocate** every creature in this cave... even the **parasites** hidden in the darkest places. He will wreak total **havoc**!"

Alex looked **embarrassed**.

"I didn't do it **deliberately**," he explained. "I tried to keep under control the food that I **ingested** last night, but it keeps wanting to **proceed** towards the exit."

"Why don't YOU **proceed** towards the exit of the cave and handle this **inconvenience**?" asked Lucy. "Go and use the toilet and come back!" she **urged** Alex **impatiently**.

"I want to use the toilet, but there is one tiny problem. THERE IS NO TOILET outside this cave! Remember? We're in the middle of nowhere! We're surrounded by trees," clarified Alex.

"Then, go and use a tree!" Lucy was growing more **impatient**. She was **terrified** by the thought that Alex would let loose again with something even louder and smellier.

"But I have no toilet paper!" whined Alex.

"You'll be fine!" Lucy tried to encourage him. "You can use leaves and grass, just like our cavemen ancestors did. Maybe you'll be **fortunate** and find a squirrel."

"I don't get it." Alex was **baffled**. "What does a squirrel have to do with anything?

"The fur of the squirrel is softer than the leaves," explained Danny.

Alex gave Lucy a **hostile** look.

"First of all: eew! Second, even if I do go to handle this **inconvenience** outside of this cave, I still won't know how to find you when I get back," insisted Alex.

"How could you lose us? There's only one way in and one way out of this cave!" said Lucy.

"I'll come with you," said Danny. He couldn't leave his friend when he needed him the most.

"Thanks, Danny. You're a life saver."

Alex was too embarrassed to tell Cristina about his **inconvenience**. He and Danny decided to sneak out **discreetly** and **proceed** towards the exit of the cave.

CHAPTER 39

The **Accident**

Alex **settled** his **unsettling inconvenience** behind a large tree. He came out with a large, **satisfied** smile on his face.

"Look at you, all happy and giggly!" Danny greeted his friend. "I **assume** the battle is over and the **epic** saga had a happy ending."

"It did for me," confirmed Alex. "But we'd better run before the root of that tree **decomposes** and the whole thing falls over!"

"Why? Did you **infest** the **environment** that badly? It's not like you poured acid at the bottom of the tree trunk, is it?" asked Danny.

"It **certainly** felt like I did," Alex explained. "Let's get back inside. I don't want to take any chances."

"Good idea," said Danny.

The two boys entered the **gloomy** cave and **descended** towards the chamber where they had left the rest of the group. Danny took out his tiny flashlight. The light was dim, but it was good enough for the two boys to find their way back.

"It's so cold in this cave! My ears feel as cold as these **stalactites**," said Alex after a while.

"Here we go again." Danny was getting **exasperated** by his friend whining about everything. "Dude, you should have brought a hat if you knew that your ears would be sensitive to the cold."

"I didn't bring hats with me in the camp. I don't wear hats. At all. Not since my skiing **accident**," explained Alex.

"Skiing **accident**?" Danny started to feel a little bit **embarrassed** by his lack of empathy. "What happened to you?"

"Oh, something terrible. It's very painful to **recall** the **events**," said Alex with a **gloomy demeanor**.

"Oh, poor soul!" Danny was feeling more and more sorry for his friend. "Did you get badly **injured**?"

"No, not at all," said Alex **abruptly**.

Danny's **demeanor** indicated that he did not expect this answer. He was **baffled**.

"Then what happened?"

"Well, last year, when I went skiing with my family, we took a short bus ride to the slopes. On the bus, we met a very nice lady," Alex started his story.

"Let me guess: She wasn't so nice after all! She tried to trip you on the slopes!" Danny interrupted his friend **abruptly**.

"No, she was very nice from the beginning to the end," said Alex.

"Then what happened?" Danny was more and more **intrigued**.

"The lady started to talk to me about things that I liked, and I didn't like. Then, she asked me whether I wanted a cream-filled milk chocolate."

"And?" Danny was getting **impatient**. "What happened to you?"

"I was wearing my hat in that moment. The hat covered my ears and because of that, I couldn't hear her question. So, I just put a dumb smile on my face, and I didn't say anything. Anything at all! **Eventually**, the lady turned around and gave the chocolate to another kid."

"That was it?" asked Danny.

"Yes! Can you believe it? Ever since that **accident**, I promised myself that I would never again wear a hat."

"I see how that could be very traumatic for you," said Danny **sarcastically**.

"It was! Who would give up on a cream-filled milk chocolate like that?"

"Not the Alex I know!" said Danny with a giggle. Then, pointing towards a large **stalactite** he **abruptly** changed the subject of their conversation. "If I **recall** correctly, as soon as we pass this **stalactite**, we should see the chamber and rejoin our group."

Danny was right. Sort of. Immediately after the boys passed the **stalactite**, they reached the chamber and rejoined ... no one. The room was **gloomy** and empty. The group was gone!

CHAPTER 40

The Light

"How could they leave without us?" wondered Alex in **disbelief.** "It's **abnormal** to leave two kids walking around in a **gloomy** cave all by themselves. What if we get **injured**?"

"Dude, relax!" Danny was trying to **appease** his friend. "As Lucy said, there is one way in and one way out. What could possibly happen to us?"

"I don't know – maybe we freeze to death and turn into a **stalagmite**? Wait a minute…" Alex's **demeanor** changed from **anxious** to **terrified**. "What if these **stalagmites** are actually children who froze to death in this cave? Let's get out of here!" exclaimed Alex, **horrified** by the idea that he, too, might become a **stalagmite**.

"What do you **suggest** we do?" asked Danny **impatiently**. "Go back outside and wait in front of the cave? And smell the fresh air? I guess we can't do that now, can we?"

Alex thought for a few seconds and then **agreed** that Danny had made a good point.

"I guess it's more **appealing** to explore the cave than to wait outside and enjoy the … freshness of the **rural** breeze. Let's go ahead and find our group!"

The two boys **proceeded** forward. The dim beam of Danny's flashlight was **certainly** not **adequate** for cave exploration, but it helped them avoid the various obstacles. It was **certainly** better than Alex's non-existent flashlight. The boys followed a narrow trail until they reached a point where something unexpected happened: the trail split in two.

"So much for only one way in and one way out!" **grumbled** Alex.

"Hey, look, there's a light ahead. I think we found our group!" said Danny with a **relieved demeanor**.

"Great! Just in time!" Alex was **relieved**, too. When he had first noticed the split, he began to feel **anxious**. He **disliked** the idea of having to decide which route to take, without any clues. But now, the light shining in front of them made him feel more at **ease**.

The two boys took the trail on the right and headed towards the light. Danny was leading, with the flashlight beam pointed to the ground in front of them. Suddenly, the beam of light flickered twice before disappearing altogether.

"Danny, what are you doing? Keep the flashlight pointed to the ground – I can't see anything!" said Alex as he started to stumble.

"My flashlight battery just died!" exclaimed Danny. "Fortunately, we are very close. Put your hand on my shoulder, and I'll lead you."

The two boys headed towards the light in front of them.

"Hello!" said Danny. "Guys, we're here!"

Nobody answered.

The two boys **proceeded** towards the light.

"Hello! Is anybody here?" asked Danny.

Again, no answer.

As the two boys **approached** the source of light, they soon realized that it was a lit candle. A good old-fashioned candle, which was fairly **intact**. That meant that whoever had lit it, had done so very recently. That was the good news. The group should not be too far ahead. The bad news was that there was nobody to be seen.

"Where are they?" wondered Danny. "I'm sure they left the candle here for us, to help guide our way, but where could they be?"

Alex lifted the candle and started to explore the cave.

"I'm sure they can't be far," he said. "It's really **fortunate** that we have this light. Without it, we would be in complete darkness!"

"Be careful with that," warned Danny. "I don't have any matches or a lighter."

"Me, neither," said Alex. He started to grow a little bit **unsettled** when he realized how fragile their only source of light was. Even the smallest breeze could blow out the candle and leave them in complete darkness.

"I guess I should better... " Alex didn't get to finish his sentence. He was getting nervous. And when he got nervous like that, he always...

"Achoo!" Alex sneezed over the candle, and the light was gone.

CHAPTER 41

The Trap

"Did you just blow out the candle?" asked Danny in **disbelief**. "Did you think it was your birthday?"

Alex couldn't say a word. His brain refused to accept what had just happened, really happened. He was hoping it was all a **nightmare**, and he would wake up very soon. But that did not happen.

The darkness was **pervasive**. The boys were **horrified**.

"Hello!" yelled Alex. "Is anybody there?"

Total silence.

"How about we carefully continue walking down this path? I'm sure we'll find them," **suggested** Danny. "We must find them! Why would anybody light the candle if not to lead us towards the group?"

"You're right! It's the only **hypothesis** that makes any sense," agreed Alex. "Let's continue walking slowly on this path."

Danny stretched his left arm in front of him and **proceeded** forward while constantly keeping his right hand on the cave wall. Alex was holding his friend and following him very closely. They stumbled but managed to keep their balance. Progress was slow, and it took them half an hour just to **advance** slightly deeper into the cave. They had to walk very carefully and assume that every step they made could lead them into a pit or a puddle. **Fortunately**, so far the trail was flat and dry.

The boys continued to **advance** until Danny suddenly gasped.

"What is it?" asked Alex. "Do you see a light?"

"No," said Danny with an **anguished** voice.

"Then, what is it?" asked Alex **impatiently**.

Danny was **shivering**, and not because he was cold. His Barbie doll outfit was keeping him warm enough. He started to shake even harder as he was pushing his hands forward, like he would push somebody. Or something. **Eventually,** Danny explained.

"There is a wall in front of me. I think we've reached the end of the cave."

"What do you mean, *a wall*? That's non-sense. Why would anybody light a candle to guide us to a dead-end, unless…" Alex's voice started to fade as soon as he understood what this could mean. He suddenly formed a new **hypothesis**.

"It was a trap!" both boys yelled at the same time.

CHAPTER 42

Choo Choo Train

The cave was dark and **frigid**. The boys were **shivering**, **terrified** by the thought that nobody would come rescue them, because nobody even knew where they were. Their future looked **gloomy**. Could they find their way back **uninjured**? Could they find their way back at all? Who did this to them? And why? Who could be so evil and **devious**?

"Do you think whoever **deceived** us today is the same prankster that has been playing tricks on us since we first came to camp?" asked Alex.

"Who else could it be?" replied Danny.

"I bet it's Lucy!" said Alex.

"If it's her, why did she **deliberately** tell us to bring flashlights? Why was she so **determined** to warn us about packing warm clothes? And if she was so **eager** to see us suffering, why would she care enough to share her extra clothes with us? It just doesn't not make any sense!" concluded Danny.

"None of this makes any sense," Alex **agreed**. "Come on, let's find our way back! I'd rather be in front of the cave and smell my gift to Mother Nature than stay here."

"You're right!" **agreed** Danny. "In fact, if we're lucky enough, we might even find our way back out of the cave by following that smell!"

Danny took the lead again. He turned around and slowly **proceeded** forward, guided by the cave walls. Alex was Danny's **satellite**, hanging on to his Barbie doll t-shirt. The shirt was still **intact**, but probably wouldn't be for long.

The boys **advanced** carefully and slowly. An hour must have passed since they had decided to return. Or maybe just a few minutes? Or three hours? It was impossible to estimate. It felt like time was standing still.

Danny stopped. The wall that he was using for guidance was not dry anymore. It felt wet and **slimy**. When had the cave walls become **slimy**?! He wiped his hand on his shorts and decided to get down on his knees. Alex followed him. The two boys continued to **advance** by crawling on the ground, but something was different. It did not feel like they were following a path anymore. It felt more like they had reached an open area in the cave.

"Hey, Alex! I think we're back in the chamber!" yelled Danny.

His voice thundered, and he could hear his echo. Yes, they were definitely back in the chamber. That means that the wet and **slimy** surface he touched must have been one of the **stalagmites** they had admired earlier. Back when his flashlight was still working. Good memories.

Suddenly, the two boys heard a **shriek** and saw multiple beams of lights moving **swiftly** towards them. They could hear Lucy's voice loud and clear. She sounded **relieved** and thrilled.

"I think I found them!"

The chamber was **instantaneously** flooded with light as the beams of several flashlights pointed towards Danny and Alex. The two boys were still in a crawling position.

"Boys, we've been looking all over for you! What are you doing down there?" Lucy's voice thundered. "Praying to the **stalactite** goddess? Or are you playing Choo Choo Train? Aren't you too old for that? Seriously! Should I get you a sand box, my baby friends?"

Lucy loved **embarrassing** them, but she definitely was not the prankster. She cared for them. She wouldn't want to see them hurt. Who else would lead a group of kids to rescue the two boys? Who else would sound so thrilled when she found them?

"We're happy to see you, too, Lucy," said Danny getting up.

"I can't believe I'm saying this, but I really missed you and your **compliments**," added Alex.

CHAPTER 43

By the River

Danny and Alex **rejoined** the group safely. They learned from Lucy that she had worked very hard to keep Alex's secret, **refraining** from telling Christina about their departure from the cave. But once she realized that the boys had been missing for a long time, she decided to organize a search rescue team to look for them. Luckily, the team had found the boys just in time! Now, equipped with powerful flashlights (and well-charged batteries), the group was able to return quickly to the depths of the cave, where they met back up with the other kids.

The rest of the cave exploration was thoroughly **spectacular**. At one point, the group reached a place where a waterfall streamed down from the ceiling into an underground river. The sound was very **soothing**, and the rushing water made the **environment** look like it was from another planet. The ceiling was covered with **icicles**, and they could see pockets of light shining through them. Further down, they noticed several **stalagmites** and **stalactites joining** to form a **spectacular** curtain of ice! What an incredible sight!

The cave visit ended several hours later. As the group exited the cave, the instructors began looking for a place to have a picnic.

"Let's go down there by the river," said Christina. "I don't know why, but I don't like how this place smells anymore," she added. "Maybe the air will be cleaner down there."

Danny and Alex chuckled. *It **certainly** will*, they thought. They followed the group and **settled** on a boulder by the river. They were about to unpack their lunches when Danny **noticed** Lucy heading towards the woods. She was looking for a couple of branches to make a tent out of her blanket.

"Lucy! Come here and **join** our **feast**!" yelled Danny.

Lucy did not answer. Probably she did not hear him.

"Lucy, come back! You don't want to go that way!" added Danny when he **noticed** that Lucy was heading towards a large tree. A tree that was very familiar to Alex and Danny. A tree that Alex had visited several hours ago.

It was too late. Lucy was too far away. She disappeared behind the tree.

Danny and Alex looked at each other in total silence. At first, they **refrained** from making any comments. No words were necessary. However, they could each tell from the other's **demeanor** that both boys were thinking the same thing.

Eventually, Alex muttered, "What are the chances she will..."

Alex did not get the chance to finish his sentence before his words were interrupted by a **shriek**.

"Eew! Eew! **Triple** Eew!" Lucy came out of the woods yelling and shaking her left shoe. She looked **enraged** and **disgusted**.

"Alex, I think your gift to Mother Nature was collected by one of Lucy's shoes," said Danny.

"Oh man!" Alex was **embarrassed** at first. Then, his **demeanor** changed. A **devious smirk** began taking shape on his face. He had an idea.

"Hey, Lucy, are you still hungry? That thing on your shoe looks **disgusting**, don't you think? It kind of makes you lose your **appetite**, right? Can I have your sandwich?"

CHAPTER 44

The **Hailstorm**

It was getting late in the afternoon. The kids were returning to the camp, hiking on an open dirt road. The road was **adjacent** to the river that would **eventually** lead them to the camp. **Fortunately**, the sun was hidden behind the clouds. The shade was welcome. Walking back to the camp for two hours in the blazing sun would have been a **horrific** experience.

Of course, as the kids knew very well by now, all good things **eventually** come to an end. In this case, it started with the clouds growing darker. The first drop of rain touched Danny on his cheek just when Alex was explaining to his friend his new theory about the evolution of vampires.

"Alex, I'm sorry to say this, but please don't spit on people when you talk! It's **disgusting**!" said Danny wiping his cheek.

Alex was **baffled**. He didn't think that he had spat on his friend. He chose to be quiet for a while.

Three more drops touched Danny's face.

"Dude, how can you do that?" Danny was getting **exasperated**. "How can you spit even when you're not talking?"

It didn't take him too long to figure out the answer to his question as a heavy rain began falling almost **instantaneously**. The kids were soaking wet before they could even think about finding shelter. Everybody else scattered into the forest, but Danny and Alex could not see why they would do that. They were soaked anyway. Things couldn't possibly get worse, right?

Wrong! Soon, the rain became a **hailstorm**. Walnut-sized chunks of **hail** came down, hitting the boys hard and steadily!

"Ouch! That hurts!" yelled Alex, now looking desperately for shelter.

"Argh! Yikes!" **shrieked** Danny. "I didn't order a head massage this afternoon!"

"Me neither! Where should we go?" asked Alex visibly

disturbed.

Danny **noticed** something in the distance.

"Look, there's a bridge ahead!" yelled Danny. "Let's hide under that!" he said, running towards it.

The two boys raced **chaotically** towards the bridge. Danny was the first to **descend** the riverbank. Just as he was about to dive underneath the bridge, something stopped him.

"Umm, Alex," he said in a faint voice.

"Danny, I don't have time for a chat now!" yelled Alex, trying to **descend** the riverbank. The earth was muddy and slippery. He had already lost his balance a few times and was now trying hard to make it down the riverbank without falling. "I can barely keep my balance... What? What is it?" Alex had just **noticed** his friend's **demeanor**, which appeared to be saying '*Oops*'!

Danny **grumbled**, "Alex, we're not alone."

CHAPTER 45

Under the Bridge

Alex **descended** the riverbanks. He **glanced** under the bridge and **instantaneously** realized why his friend was looking so **baffled**.

"Hey, who parked all these sheep here?" he asked Danny. "There's no room left under this bridge!"

Indeed, **numerous** sheep were lying under the bridge in a huddle. There must have been several dozen! They were all dry and happy. Unlike Danny and Alex. With the **hailstorm** continuing to strike **ferociously**, the boys had to come up with an **effective** plan.

Alex picked up a sheep and told Danny, "Hey, let's make some room here! Grab a sheep!"

"Are you insane?" asked Danny. "These sheep could be **infested** with fleas – remember?"

"Who cares about fleas, now?" replied Alex. "If I must choose between **hail** knocking me on the head and fleas biting my butt, I prefer the fleas. My head is much more valuable and needs protection. Plus, I don't think fleas have much **appetite** in this kind of weather.

I'm sure they'll try to stay as close as possible to the sheep's skin. I can't imagine any of them saying, *I'm bored. Let's go out and eat! What do we have on the menu? Hmm, look at that. Alex's butt looks delicious. I think I'll have some of that. Medium rare, please.*"

Danny laughed in spite of himself, and he had to admit that his friend's **hypothesis** made sense. Even if the sheep had fleas, he doubted they would be up and bouncing right now. Plus, the kids would drop their clothes and take a long, hot shower the moment they arrived back at camp. What a glorious moment that would be! The thought of a hot shower was very **appealing**.

Danny **glanced** around at the sheep and found a big one that was sleeping peacefully. It looked like a big pile of wool. *This is it*, he thought. *If I'm **swift** enough, the sheep will barely know what happened to her. By the time she opens her eyes, she'll be out in the rain, and I'll be enjoying my **hail**-free shelter.*

With a quick move, Danny put his hands on the sheep and yanked **vigorously**. To his surprise, the sheep was much, much lighter than he expected. How was that possible? Danny looked at the pile of wool in his hands and quickly realized that he was not holding a sheep in his arms. He was only holding the wool. Had he just skinned the sheep alive?!?

Danny was **terrified**. What had he done? He **glanced** back under the bridge and the **horrifying** reality struck him even harder than the **hail** had. He felt like he might **faint**. What he saw was worse than his worst **nightmare**. His deep sense of **dread** made him feel completely numb to the **hailstorm**. He was shocked!

The pile of wool had not been covering a sheep. It had been covering a shepherd. But not just any shepherd. It was the same **solitary** shepherd that the boys had met two days ago. The **solitary** shepherd that believed the boys had wanted to eat his sheep. The shepherd whose peaceful sleep had just been **disturbed** by Danny yanking off his coat. Yes, the pile of wool was the shepherd's coat! It was the coat that he used as a blanket to keep him warm during his afternoon nap under the bridge.

The **solitary** shepherd opened one eye. Then he opened the other one. He saw Danny holding his coat. He saw Alex holding a sheep under his arm. He **grumbled** loudly.

Danny wished he had skinned a sheep alive. That thought would have been less **horrifying** than this new reality. How could he explain to the shepherd that he was not trying to steal his coat? How could he explain to the shepherd that Alex was not trying to steal his sheep? All Danny could do was turn to Alex and say one word.

"Run!"

CHAPTER 46

Deserted

Danny and Alex did not care about the storm anymore. They did not care about the walnut-sized **hail** massaging their heads, backs, arms and legs. They did not care about the lightning they had suddenly **noticed** in the distance. They did not even seem to hear the sounds of thunder cracking nearby. All they could hear was the sloshing of their soaked shoes hitting the ground **ferociously** as they ran like they had never run before.

"Is he following us?" asked Alex between gasps, without turning his head.

"I don't know!" yelled Danny in **anguish**. "Do you want me to stop, go back, and ask him if he is chasing us? Maybe ask him if he still has some pork skin left for you to chew? Do you feel the need for a snack now?"

"Well, just turn your head and look behind us," **suggested** Alex.

"I'm not doing that. I'm kind of busy saving my life," explained Danny without slowing down. "Why don't you do that?"

"I'm in the middle of something, too," replied Alex as he began catching even more speed.

The boys ran all the way to the camp. **Fortunately**, by the time they **arrived** there, the rain and hail had stopped. It was only after they crossed the bridge that led to the camp that they finally found the courage to look back over their shoulders. They didn't see anybody behind them. The shepherd and his **gloomy demeanor** were out of sight. What a relief! They were safe!

Danny and Alex crossed the **deserted** camp all the way to cabin number eight. They didn't see anybody else around, so apparently, they were the first to return from the trip. They grabbed some dry clothes and towels from the cabin. Then, they walked across the camp, heading straight to the building where all the showers were located. Yes, that moment had finally arrived! The moment they had been waiting since those first pieces of **hail** had knocked them in the head!

Their well-deserved showers were long and hot, healing all their bruises and warming the boys up. What a **soothing** experience! A visit to a spa would have not been more relaxing than this moment. Really, it was relaxing and **entertaining** at the same time, if we consider Alex's off-tune singing and Danny's loud **gargles**.

Danny finished his shower first. He opened the door of the shower stall, ready to take his towel and clothes from the bench **adjacent** to the stall. He couldn't find his belongings. He suddenly became **suspicious**!

"Alex, did you see my stuff?"

"What stuff?"

"My towel and my clothes. All of my clothes, to be more **precise**," explained Danny.

"Oh yeah, they are underneath my clothes," explained Alex from behind the closed door of his shower stall. He was still showering.

"That's a **relief**," said Danny. "For a moment I thought that somebody had stolen them. So, could you please tell me where your clothes are?"

"Sure, I put them on the bench next to the shower stalls," explained Alex.

Danny's face dropped.

"Alex, there is only one bench here, but there is nothing on it."

Alex turned the water off. He said, "I think this water got into my ears and is making me hear crazy things. For a moment, I thought I heard you saying that you don't see my clothes."

"That's exactly what I said," confirmed Danny.

"Do you mean you don't see my Mickey Mouse watch either?" asked Alex in **disbelief**.

"No, Alex. I don't see your clothes, and I don't see your Mickey Mouse watch either," explained Danny.

Alex exited the stall and looked at the bench. It was **deserted**, just like the camp was. Or at least, just as **deserted** as they thought the camp was. Apparently, the boys were wrong about that last part. Their clothes were gone, and somebody else was in the camp playing pranks on them. *Again!*

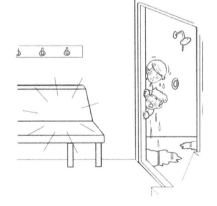

CHAPTER 47

Caution

Danny and Alex walked outside **cautiously**. They wrapped themselves around the waist and all the way down to their knees with toilet paper, so they wouldn't be completely naked. They didn't want to **expose** themselves out in the open knowing that somebody was watching them. Who knew what **devious** plan the prankster had in mind?

Fortunately, as they stepped outside, they didn't see anybody. No prankster laughing at them. The camp looked as **deserted** as it had several minutes ago when they first crossed it to go to the showers. But the boys knew that they had to be very **cautious**. They looked left and right before **eventually proceeding** towards their cabin.

After a few steps, Danny stopped. He saw something.

"Alex, look over there! Is that a dog?"

"Yes," confirmed Alex. "And he's munching ... he's munching on my clothes!" Indeed, the dog looked like he was having a **feast** munching on a pile of rags. The rags looked like they used to be clothes, in their better days.

"Alex, did you have snacks in your pockets?" asked Danny.

Alex paused for a few seconds. Then he said, "Well, after lunch I might have saved some leftover sandwiches. You know, I wanted to be **cautious**, just in case I got hungry before dinner..."

Danny looked at his friend. Then, he suddenly hugged him. Alex was totally surprised.

"Aren't you mad?" Alex asked his friend.

"I was for a second. But now I'm thrilled that the mystery is solved!"

"What do you mean?" Alex was still puzzled.

"Here's my new **hypothesis**. We don't have to worry about a prankster watching us anymore because, well...because there is no prankster! This stray dog was attracted by the smell of food coming from your clothes. He grabbed all our clothes and now he's working his way through the pockets of your pants."

"I guess I should consider myself **fortunate** that I'm not wearing those pants right now," said Alex.

The boys laughed. They felt **relieved** that there was no prankster. **Relieved** that nobody was there to see them wearing nothing but some toilet paper wrapped around their waist and upper legs. **Relieved** that there was nobody in the camp but them.

"Hey! Is that Danny and Alex?" a voice yelled behind them.

"I think it's them. But why are they wearing white skirts?" yelled another voice.

"And what are they doing hugging in the middle of the camp?" said another voice.

Danny and Alex **glanced** over their shoulders. In a split-second, they learned that three kids had just returned to camp from their field trip. In the distance, they could see more coming. Apparently, the boys' **fortune** was short-lived. They had to hurry back to their cabin before the rest of the group arrived and saw them wearing the toilet paper skirts.

"Hi guys, did you enjoy your field trip?" Danny asked. Before he could get an answer, he continued, "Well, nice chatting with you. We need to go. Bye!"

Danny and Alex **proceeded cautiously** towards their cabin. The last thing they needed was for their skirts to start ripping apart while the whole camp was watching them.

CHAPTER 48

Dilemmas

The boys from cabin number eight had a hard time falling asleep that evening. The **events** that had taken place on Thursday filled their brains with many **dilemmas**.

"Who do you think could have lit the candle in the cave? And why?" asked Alex. He was tucked in bed already, but he had taken **precautions** in case anybody tried to play a prank on them that evening. He checked that the door was locked (twice!), he moved the furniture against the door (just like he had on Monday evening!), and he hid under his pillow a flashlight and a fork that he had borrowed from the cafeteria. He was armed and ready to fight back!

"I have no idea," answered Danny. He, too, had a flashlight and three pairs of shoes under his pillow, ready to **defend** himself. If somebody entered their cabin that night, Danny could do some real damage. "The candle was almost **intact** when we got there. That means it was probably lit by somebody from our group."

"It's strange because Lucy and the other guys who rescued us said they didn't see anything," continued Alex. "Do you think they were lying to us?"

"This is a terrible **dilemma**. If that were true, then why would they come rescue us? It's possible that Lucy and the other guys didn't see the candle burning in the distance because its dim flame went **unnoticed** when the cave was flooded with the light of many powerful flashlights," explained Danny. "It's like when you look at the stars at night: when you're in the city, surrounded by many artificial lights, you only see a handful of stars. But when you're out in the country, in complete darkness, there seem to be millions of stars in the sky."

"How about a mysterious prankster that is not part of our group?" asked Alex.

"You mean somebody who lives in this area? Somebody who knows a secret entrance to the cave? Somebody who followed us from a distance?" Danny thought for a few seconds. "Hmm… that could be a good **hypothesis**. Maybe there is a stranger that watches every move we make."

"It does make sense, doesn't it?" asked Alex. "In all honesty, I'm not convinced that the dog stole our clothes."

"What makes you say that?" Danny was **baffled**. "The **evidence** was pretty clear."

"The only **evidence** we had was that the dog was munching on our clothes. We can't be **certain** that it was the dog or somebody else that took our clothes. If the **evidence** was so clear, why couldn't I find my Mickey Mouse watch?" asked Alex. "When we went back to pick up our clothes - or whatever was left of them - we could find everything except for my watch."

"Maybe the dog ate it!" Danny tried to **ease** his friend's **suspicion**.

"Do dogs eat watches?" asked Alex **abruptly**. "I can't remember reading any signs posted in front of the houses saying, *Beware of dogs. They will eat your watches*, or *No trespassing. This* *property is guarded by a watch-loving dog."*

"I meant, by accident," clarified Danny.

"By accident or not, I'm not going to solve this **dilemma** by chasing that dog and looking in his poop to see whether he **ingested**, and then **eventually** released my watch."

"Well, maybe this is the kind of **dilemma** that cannot be solved," concluded Danny. "All we can do now is continue to be **cautious**. We have one more full day in this camp. Remember, on Saturday morning the bus will be here to pick us up."

"I guess you're right," **grumbled** Alex. "One more day. We can make it," he added. **Eventually** he fell asleep, still gripping his fork tightly.

CHAPTER 49

Friday

Danny and Alex woke up the next morning **uninjured**. Nobody had entered their cabin during the night. Alex had not **accidentally** stabbed himself with the fork while he was asleep. Danny was not **suffocated** by the smell of his shoes. He was just a little bit pale and confused when he woke up with some shoelaces in his mouth, but soon he **recalled** the previous day's **endeavors** and his resulting plan of **defense**.

The boys went to breakfast wondering whether anybody knew what had really happened to them the day before. After they got their food and sat at the table, they **glanced** around the cafeteria. Nobody looked at them **suspiciously**. Maybe the three kids that had seen them wearing the toilet paper around their waists had not **exposed** their **embarrassing** story. That was a good sign. Then, Lucy came and sat at their table.

"Hey, I heard that you went shopping yesterday. Is that true? When did you have time to do that?" she asked.

Danny and Alex were **baffled**. "What?"

Lucy continued. "I always wanted to have a long, white skirt. Where did you find those in the middle of nowhere?"

The boys finally understood where the conversation was going, and the outcome looked **gloomy**. Obviously, they were wrong about the three kids keeping their secret. Danny and Alex had to come up with a good excuse before Lucy started talking loudly about this.

"Shh. Don't say it out loud," said Danny shaking his head **vigorously**, hoping to make her understand that she would be making the biggest mistake of her life if she **revealed** a well-hidden secret. "Those were not skirts. Those were robes. You know, the ones that the ancient Romans wore. We made them out of the bedsheets. We were practicing for a play. It's supposed to be a surprise."

"Oh, goody! I love surprises!" whispered Lucy, excitedly. "When are you going to put on the play?"

"Tonight, during the campfire," explained Danny.

"Great! I can't wait! I'll see you then!" she said and left the boys alone to enjoy their breakfast.

Alex was **baffled**. He asked Danny, "What are we going to do now? Do you have a plan? You told Dutchee a few days ago that I would sing, during the campfire tonight, and now Lucy thinks that we'll perform some kind of play."

"We'll figure something out. I'm sure Dutchee and Lucy will be distracted and will forget all about that. If they don't, we'll just come up with a good excuse. I've heard that we have a full day ahead that includes a blueberry paintball match and an eating challenge."

"Eating challenge?" Alex's eyes sparkled.

"I have no idea what the challenge is about. I guess we'll find out soon enough."

"Where is all this going to happen?" asked Alex.

"Do you remember the two huts that we built on Tuesday afternoon?" asked Danny.

"The ones in the forest **adjacent** to the camp?"

"Yes, there. I've heard that after breakfast we'll meet at the huts to have a blueberry paintball competition, whatever that is. It sounds like a lot of fun, don't you think?"

"I sure do! As long as it doesn't involve a **harness** and a **carabiner**, I'm cool with it. Actually, anything involving food, including blueberries, sounds awesome to me!" admitted Alex.

"Dude, your **perennial** hunger is truly **epic**," said Danny to his friend. "After camp is over, every meal I eat is going to remind me of you."

The two boys continued enjoying their breakfast. As usual, they were totally **oblivious** to what was going to happen in the forest that day.

CHAPTER 50

Blueberry Paintball

After breakfast, all the kids met in the forest. They were divided into two teams that were expected to compete against each other. Each participant received a t-shirt, a spit-powered launcher, and a container with blueberries. One team had yellow t-shirts and the other team had white t-shirts. The headquarters of the teams were the two huts. From there, each team would plan out an attack strategy against the other team. The participants from one team were expected to hunt the participants of the other team and use the launcher to shoot blueberries towards them. If the hit was strong enough, it would leave a stain on their competitor's t-shirts. Just like a paintball game, but with blueberries. The team that put the most stains on their opposing team's t-shirts, would win the game!

The battle started. Danny and Alex were on the team with yellow shirts. After a brief strategic meeting in the hut with their teammates, the two boys were chosen to **defend** an area of the forest that spread from their hut all the way down to the river. Their role was **crucial** in providing an **adequate defense** of their headquarters and **exposing** all the sneaky attackers that would try to make them surrender.

Danny and Alex carried out their task very **effectively**. They hid behind two fallen trees located **remotely** from one another, covered themselves with leaves, and waited. Soon, the competitors from the other team started to show up. **Unfortunately** for them, they did not stand a chance. Danny and Alex welcomed them with a blueberry shower that rained down on them heavily. The kids from the white-shirted team were taken by surprise. Their shirts turned dark blue **instantaneously**, but the worst thing was that they could not see where the blueberries were flying from. Some of the kids hid behind the trees, but that strategy did not work either. No matter how hard they tried, they were **exposed** to either Danny or Alex. The two boys wreaked **havoc** among their opponents. Eventually, their competitors had to run away, **repelled** by this **vigorous defense**.

After this success, Danny and Alex waited what felt like an **eternity**, but nobody else **approached** them. The other team had probably figured out by then that they were fighting against very **effective** shooters and had become very **cautious**. They didn't want to take any more chances. So what should the two boys do? They grew **impatient**. Their pile of blueberries was far from being **depleted**. The boys were ready to do more damage, but they had no target. This presented them with a **dilemma**. On the one hand, they were supposed to just sit and wait. But on the other hand, what if their team needed them someplace else?

Danny and Alex decided to **proceed** towards the enemy headquarters. They decided to sneak by the riverbanks and to surround their perimeter. This way, they could attack their competitors from behind and take them by surprise!

The two boys **advanced** for a few minutes before Alex **noticed** something **abnormal**. He stopped Danny.

"Hey, look at those bushes! Did you see something moving?" he whispered to his friend.

"Now that you mention it, I thought I saw something moving. But I can't see anything past them," replied Danny.

"I think there's somebody there," said Alex. The bushes moved again. There was clearly somebody there.

The boys smiled.

"Let's greet our opponent **properly** with a blueberry shower!" said Alex excitedly. "If it's going to rain, let it pour!"

Each boy armed his launcher with twenty blueberries. They wanted their shot to be as **effective** as possible. The competitor wouldn't stand a chance, particularly if he or she were **approached** from two different angles. Nobody could be **immune** to a sudden well-coordinated attack from two sides.

Danny and Alex coordinated themselves using hand signals. They **approached** the bush **discreetly**. They were ready. The boys counted to three and then jumped behind the bush, discharging all their blueberries.

Just as the boys had **predicted**, the person behind the bush was taken by surprise. His white shirt **instantaneously** changed color. His **demeanor** showed that he was stunned. He could not say a word. He could not move a limb. He just watched in **disbelief** as he was covered head to toe in something blue and **slimy**. The attack was very **effective**.

There was only one problem. The victim was not a kid from the camp. The victim was not a kid at all. It was the **solitary** shepherd.

CHAPTER 51

The Gift

The shepherd looked at the kids in **disbelief.** Then, he looked at the **disgusting slimy** thing on his shirt. What was it? What had just happened?

"You..." he **grumbled**. He tried to continue his sentence, but a pork skin that was hanging from the corner of his mouth fell on the ground. That was a shame, because the skin looked like it was fresh. Definitely not older than two days.

"You made me drop my lunch!" the shepherd continued.

The kids froze. They **refrained** from making a sound. They **refrained** from making a move. They **refrained** from breathing for a while. They tried very hard to remain **stoic**.

The shepherd continued, "You ruined my beauty sleep!"

Danny and Alex **glanced** at his unshaved beard, his heavily wrinkled face, and his **gloomy demeanor**. How long would he need to sleep to reach the beauty stage?

The shepherd added, "You ruined my shirt!"

The kids thought about explaining that the shirt was not really *completely* **deteriorated**, and that the stains would easily wash away, but they were too **terrified** to say anything. They took a step back. **Unfortunately**, the shepherd's sheep were lying down in the sun just behind them. The kids did not see the sheep when they backed up. Danny stepped on one of them. The sheep got up and answered with a strong "baa" followed by another one with a loud "meh". The unexpected sounds and movement took the boys by surprise. They lost their balance and fell on two of the sheep. The animals did not move. Maybe they liked having the boys sitting on them. Or maybe they were dead.

"You broke my sheep!" yelled the increasingly **enraged** shepherd. His **precious** sheep eventually moved. They were not broken. They were just surprised.

The shepherd looked at the kids and said, "You...You..."

Suddenly his eyes sparkled when he caught sight of Alex's container of blueberries. Then he licked his shirt. Sure enough, it tasted like blueberry!

"You brought me blueberries? They are my favorite! How did you know?" the shepherd asked excitedly. His **demeanor** changed dramatically.

Alex was about to explain, "Actually, these blueberries are ..."

Danny interrupted him **abruptly**, "They are all for you! Here, we have two containers! Take them both!"

"Two containers? All for me? Thank you so much!" The shepherd was thrilled. "But what are they for?"

"They are for being a very friendly neighbor," explained Danny. "We love bringing gifts to our neighbors!"

"That is so nice," the shepherd said. "But I need to be honest with you. Around here, when we bring gifts, we don't spit them in people's faces and on their clothes. We have different customs."

Alex tried to explain again, "Actually, we don't...."

Danny interrupted him again, shaking him **vigorously**, "What my friend is trying to say is that where we come from, we don't just give away the gifts. We first spit them. Isn't that what everybody does?"

"No, not around here," said the shepherd with a serious **demeanor**.

"Well, now we know. We'll try to remember that, right Alex?"

Alex agreed, nodding his head **ferociously**. He dared not speak anymore. Danny was doing a great job of getting them out of trouble.

Danny continued, "I hope you enjoy our present, and thank you again for being such a friendly neighbor. Bye-bye, now."

The two boys left as the shepherd continued waving at them, smiling pleasantly. Obviously, the shepherd did not recognize them. He did not realize that a day before they had appeared to be about to steal one of his sheep and his coat. Danny and Alex left quickly before the shepherd became **suspicious**.

CHAPTER 52

The **Disgusting** Lunch

It was lunch time. The kids from Daris Camp returned from the forest. The yellow team successfully defeated the white team, thanks to Danny and Alex. The two boys had scared their competitors so badly, that they had all decided to take an alternate route towards their enemies' headquarters. **Unfortunately** for them, the alternate route was a trap. By the time they realized that, it was too late. They were surrounded by their competitors, and soon their shirts looked anything but white! It was a glorious day for the team with yellow shirts!

All the kids were now ready to eat, and this was no **typical** lunch. It was the last lunch at Daris Camp, and the counselors made it special, by organizing an eating challenge. The meal was an open buffet, but eating the food was very challenging. No, the food was not bad. Actually, it was quite **delicious**. So what was the trick? The meals *looked* totally **disgusting**!

For appetizers, the kids had delicious ham and cheese sandwiches that were covered with a **slimy** vegetable dressing that looked like boogers. If you closed your eyes, the food would have tasted heavenly. But if you looked at the snotty bread… well, that was another story.

For entrees, the kids had **delicious** meatballs swimming in a **fabulous** puree. The food tasted amazing, but again… it looked less **appealing**. Why? The whole meal was served in a… diaper. The dish looked just like a regular diaper fully loaded with baby poop. The kids had to fight very hard against their natural **disgust** to scoop the food out and eat it.

The kids had dessert too! Cockroach cookies and skunk-tail-shaped cake. Yummy!

The main beverage was a delicious fruit punch in an enormous bowl. The punch flavor was a combination of cranberry, raspberry and cherry. It was mouthwatering! Who doesn't love a refreshing fruit punch in the middle of a hot summer day, right? Well, many people would say no even to fruit punch if they saw **numerous** eyeballs floating at the surface of the bowl. No, not real eyeballs – they were actually made out of plastic - but they looked very realistic.

Throughout the lunch, Alex was making his way through the crowd, enjoying every morsel of food he could put his hands on.

"How can you eat that?" asked Lucy.

"How can you NOT eat this?" asked Alex as he was dipping his face inside the diaper, trying to fish out the last meatball. "These meatballs taste heavenly!"

"I'm sure they would if they were served on a plate!" replied Lucy, totally **disgusted**.

"What's wrong with this plate?" asked Alex, licking up whatever was left of the puree at the bottom of the diaper.

Lucy strongly **disliked** how the lunch looked, but she was hungry. Closing her eyes, she gently removed a meatball from a diaper and tried to nibble a tiny bite.

"What are you? New at eating?" asked Alex, surprised to see her struggling to fight her **disgust**. "Meatballs are meant to be gobbled!"

"Alex, I'm sure you would eat anything, even a worm-**infested** chocolate pudding!" said Lucy.

Alex's eyes sparkled.

"Do they have chocolate pudding?" he asked.

Danny **joined** their conversation.

"No, my friend, you have to stick with the skunk-tail-shaped cake, which is **delicious** by the way," he explained.

"You boys are disgusting!" **grumbled** Lucy, leaving the cafeteria as Danny and Alex enjoyed being victorious for the second time that day.

The boys were **satisfied**. They had had a very good day! Of course, they had no clue what was going to happen that evening at the campfire.

CHAPTER 53

The Campfire

The kids from Daris Camp spent the rest of their afternoon preparing the campfire. First, they found an area that was far away from the woods and the buildings, as well as sheltered from the wind. Then, they removed all potentially flammable materials from the area, such as twigs, leaves or firewood. Next, they marked the area where the campfire would be, dug a small pit in the dirt, and circled it with rocks. They filled the pit with paper and pinecones, on top of which they built several layers of kindling, alternating direction with each layer. Finally, they placed logs together in a tepee shape. Nearby, they had two hoses connected to the main water line, just in case the fire got out of control. By the time the sun began setting, the campfire was blazing, flames soaring to the sky.

Danny and Alex, together with everybody else from the camp, gathered around the fire and enjoyed the **spectacular** dance of the flames. What a show! Some of the kids stood while others sat on giant logs around the fire. Danny and Alex couldn't find room on the logs, so they decided to sit down on the grass. They quickly learned that this was a bad idea because the grass was all wet! The boys didn't know that just before the fire was lit, the counselors had sprayed the grass with water so there wouldn't be any dry and combustible grass near the fire. Now, the boys had wet butts and a new **dilemma**.

"This feels uncomfortable," said Danny. "I need to change my pants."

"Me, too," said Alex. "But I don't have any clean clothes left. I had to change clothes every time I was around the sheep. That was three times this week! Do you have any extra pants?"

"No, I actually wanted to ask you the same question because I have run out of clean clothes, too. This is my last pair of pants," answered Danny, visibly concerned.

"What should we do? Here in the mountains, it gets cold quickly, and I don't want to get sick," said Alex.

"How about we let the campfire dry our pants?" asked Danny.

"What do you suggest? We should just stick our butts out towards the fire and act like everything is normal? Don't you think people will start wondering how we got our pants wet? Before we knew it, everybody would be saying that we peed our pants."

"No, I have a better idea. Let's dance!"

Alex had to admit that Danny's idea was not bad. Being an enthusiastic camper and dancing around the **spectacular** campfire was not really *that* **abnormal**. All they had to do was find the right dance moves to get their butts close enough to the fire to dry off.

The boys started to dance. Just as they had **predicted**, everyone appreciated their enthusiasm. Some kids even joined them. Slowly but surely, the boys brought their wet pants closer to the fire. It felt so good! The good news was that their pants started to dry very quickly. The bad news was that their pants dried a little *too* quickly.

At first, there was just light smoke and an **atypical** smell. Then, the boys felt a burning sensation. Finally, they looked at each other and when they realized what had happened, they started **shrieking instantaneously**, "Our pants are on fire!"

The boys took off their jackets and t-shirts and started to slap their butts, screaming. Their screams attracted Lucy's attention. She **recalled** the conversation she had had with them that morning. She got excited to see their performance!

"Attention, everyone! Attention, everyone! Attention, everyone!" she yelled as loudly as she could. "Alex and Danny have prepared a play for us tonight. It's a surprise! Let's respect their hard work and watch their act!"

"Yes, I remember Alex practicing his song several days ago," added Dutchee. "Let's give them a round of applause!"

Everyone clapped and turned their attention to Danny and Alex. The audience cheered as the boys threw their arms and feet in the air **chaotically**. They cheered every time the boys **vigorously** slapped each other's butts with their clothes. They cheered when the boys were making animal-like sounds. They cheered when they saw the special effects of smoke coming out of the boys' pants. They even cheered when they saw the boys running towards the nearby river. But they stopped cheering when they saw the two boys jumping into the river. The only ones that were **relieved** when that happened were Danny and Alex.

CHAPTER 54

Saturday

It was the last day of camp. The bus arrived early in the morning. Everybody was getting their bags ready, and the counselors were making their last rounds before loading the bus.

Danny and Alex finished packing their bags and **proceeded** towards the meeting point to **join** the rest of the group. The two boys were still wearing their pajamas. These were the only dry and clean clothes they had left. The boys didn't mind. At least they had some clothes to wear. And they weren't even pink!

Lucy greeted the boys.

"I loved the show that you put on last night! When you become famous actors, I hope you will remember me."

"We definitely won't forget you, Lucy. When you come for our autographs, just remember to bring the pink shirts you loaned us," said Danny.

"Deal!" agreed Lucy.

Just then, the counselors announced that they were ready to load the bus. Lucy left quickly, leaving her bag behind. Alex grabbed it, trying to get it to Lucy before she got on the bus.

"Lucy, you forgot your…"

Apparently, Alex had grabbed the bag too suddenly and it fell open, spilling its contents on the ground. Among them were a half-empty jar of strawberry jam, a handful of chocolate eggs, some candles, and… a Mickey Mouse watch.

Lucy turned around when she heard Alex. She was just in time to see the boys' long faces. Just in time to understand that the new **evidence** clearly **revealed** that she had been the camp prankster all along.

CHAPTER 55

The Mystery Solved

"You... You..." Alex was so overwhelmed by frustration that he had a hard time making himself **intelligible**.

Danny helped him out.

"What my friend is trying to say is 'YOU MEAN GIRL'! Why did you do all of that to us?"

Lucy had no choice but to come clean.

"Okay, Okay, I admit it. I had a little bit of fun. I know that I gave you a hard time, because..., well, because you made it so easy! When I overheard you talking about how scared you were of vampires, I knew that I had to put my strawberry jam to good use. The show that you put on that morning was **precious**. You should have seen your faces."

"What about the gift on our door handle. That was also you?" asked Danny.

"Yes. When we looked for clues in the forest, I **noticed** that you were excited about something. So I paid attention to your discovery. Then, I saw Alex **hurtling** the sheep poop in his mouth. It was too hilarious! I couldn't help myself. So I collected some more and then ran to your cabin and left you the 'gift'. Meanwhile, I took some of the chocolate eggs that I had brought from home – just in case we ran out of food – and I pretended that the whole morning I had been busy looking for clues. That way, I didn't look **suspicious**."

"And the candle from the cave? That was still you?" asked Alex.

"Oh yes, but for that, I don't feel one bit sorry. Dude, fix your stomach issues before entering a cave! I was happy I could trick you into taking the other route, so you wouldn't **infest** that beautiful cave with your deadly stink. But then I started to feel guilty and a little bit concerned about you, so I had a change of heart."

"What about the showers? Why did you spy on us when we were in the showers and take our clothes?"

"Eew! Why would I do that? Eew! What's wrong with you? What makes you think I would do such a thing?" Lucy was **baffled**.

"You have my watch! My Mickey Mouse watch!" exclaimed Alex. "That's solid proof!"

"This watch? I found it in the forest yesterday when we were searching for firewood for the campfire. It was covered with some kind of **slimy** stuff. I asked around but nobody recognized it. So I cleaned it up with my scarf and I decided to keep it to myself."

"So, you didn't take our clothes?" asked Alex in **disbelief**.

"I honestly have no idea what you're talking about! I didn't even know that the watch was yours. Here, take it!" said Lucy, looking very trustworthy.

While Alex recovered his watch, Danny suddenly had a **devious** thought.

"Lucy, I didn't know you like wearing somebody else's saliva on your clothes."

"What? No! Eww! Again, what are you talking about?"

"The **slimy** stuff that you wiped off the watch with your scarf - that was dog saliva. Thanks for cleaning it up for Alex."

CHAPTER 56

Rejoined

The bus arrived at the airport. Danny got off and immediately saw his parents. Mrs. Pop **hurtled** over to hug her son tightly, leaving him almost breathless.

"How was the camp? Did you like it? Did you make any friends? Did you like it?"

Danny tried hard to think of an **intelligible** answer. To think of a way to explain to her about how he had started the week by jumping in the river because he had strawberry jam on his face. Or how he had continued his week by jumping in the river because he was being chased by bees. Or how he had ended the week by jumping in the river because his pants were on fire. Danny had a hard time finding a proper way to explain to his mom that he went on a rafting trip unsupervised because his counselor has been knocked in the head and fallen overboard. Or to explain to her how Lucy had shared her vomit with everybody during that trip. Danny was working hard trying to figure out a way to explain to his mom how he had been chased by a shepherd twice, and how the shepherd's **precious** sheep had **infested** the entire camp with fleas. Then, to explain how a squirrel had ended up underneath his shirt, how he had been lost in a cave, and how he had worn a toilet paper skirt after a dog snatched his clothes. He had a hard time explaining his Transylvanian saga.

In the end, all he could come up with was: "Yeah, it was fine, Mom. It was just a regular summer camp."

EPILOGUE

The airplane was about to take off. Danny stretched his feet out on the seat next to him. It was empty. Apparently, Danny was very lucky (for once!). Nobody had claimed the seat so far, and he doubted that anyone would. Danny closed his eyes and started to enjoy what was sure to be the most comfortable flight of his life.

Then, he heard a voice next to him saying, "Excuse me, I think this is my seat."

Danny opened his eyes. He recognized the voice. He recognized the woman. He recognized her hairy armpits.

GLOSSARY

Abnormal: Not normal; weird

Abruptly: Suddenly or unexpectedly

Accidental: By mistake; by chance; unexpectedly

Adequate: Good enough; acceptable

Adjacent: Next to something or someone

Advance: To move forward

Agree: To have the same opinion; **Disagree**: To have a different opinion

Anguish: Pain or suffering

Anxiety: A fear of something; worry

Appealing: Something that you like; attractive; interesting

Appease: To make peace with somebody; to agree with someone's terms

Appetite: a feeling of wanting something very much, especially food

Approach: (1) To come near someone or something or (2) to speak to someone for the first time, or request something

Arrive: To reach a destination; to end a journey

Assume: To guess; to believe something without having evidence to support it; to suppose

Attach: To put together; to join. **Detach:** To take apart; to remove

Baffled: Confused; puzzled

Boast: to brag; to show off

Carabiner: A D-shaped metal object that is used to attach two things (like a belt to a rope)

Cautious: Careful; paying attention to avoid mistakes

Certain: To be sure, to have no doubt

Chaotic: Confused; in a disorganized manner; messy

Compliment: to praise or to say something nice about somebody

Contestant: Someone participating in a competition

Crucial: Essential; very important

Deceive: To trick or to fool somebody; to lie

Decompose: To become rotten or putrefied; to break down inro different pieces

Deliberate: On purpose

Delicious: Very tasty; yummy

Deplete: Use or empty all of the available supplies or resources

Descend: To go down

Defend: To protect something or someone from an attack

Deserted: Empty of people

Deteriorate: To damage; to break down; to destroy

Determined: Wanting something very badly; ambitious

Devious: Tricky; mean; unfair; dishonest; sneaky

Demeanor: Behavior towards others; the way somebody looks and acts

Deplete: To reduce the number of supplies; to use all the resources available

Dilemma: A difficult problem; a situation when somebody needs to make a difficult choice

Diminish: To make something small; to reduce

Disbelief: Having a hard time believing in something; refusing to accept something that is real

Discreet: Careful or cautious of not sharing sensitive information

Disgusting: Nasty; unappealing; despicable

Disturb: To bother something or someone

Dreadful: Something that causes great fear or suffering

Eager: Wanting something very much; excited

Ease: To make something feel comfortable

Effective: Successful to reach a goal with minimal effort

Elegant: Fancy; graceful; stylish

Embarrassment: A feeling of shame or awkwardness

Endeavor: An attempt to do something; an action that takes effort to reach a goal

Enormous: Very big; huge

Enrage: To make someone very angry

Entertainment: An event that people see as amusing, joyful or interesting; a show

Environment: The surroundings or the territory where someone lives

Epic: A heroic story that typically describes legendary actions of famous people from the past

Eternity: Something that lasts forever

Event: An important activity (like a concert or a party)

Eventually: In the end; finally

Evidence: Proof; facts that demonstrate whether a statement is true

Exasperate: To annoy, to frustrate somebody; to get on people's nerves

Exhausted: Very tired

Expand: To become larger in size

Exposed: Not hidden

Faint: To pass out

Fascinated: Amazed; impressed

Feast: A large meal that is usually served during a special event

Ferocious: Rough, fierce, cruel or violent

Flexible: Something (or someone) that bends easily

Fortunate: Lucky; blessed

Frigid: Cold

Gargle: To wash or rinse the mouth of throat by pushing air through a liquid

Glance: To take a peek or a quick look

Gloomy: (1) A dark place or (2) A very sad or depressed person

Grateful: Thankful; showing appreciation

Grumble: To complain or whine about something in a low-pitched voice

Gullible: Someone who is too trusty and easily tricked

Hail: Frozen rain; pieces of ice falling down from the sky. **Hailstorm:** A storm of hail

Harness: A safety equipment; a set of straps that keeps a climber attached to something

Havoc: Devastation; destruction

Hilarious: Very funny

Hive: A nest of bees

Horrified: Shocked; filled with horror

Host: A person who receives and entertains guests; a plant or an animal where a parasite lives

Hostile: Unfriendly or aggressive

Hurtle: To rush

Hypothesis: A reasonable, educated guess; an assumption that relies on facts, and yet, not proven to be true

Icicle: A handing piece of ice, formed by dripping water

Immune: Resistant or protected against danger

Impatient: Restless; without patience

Inconvenience: A problem; a difficulty that creates discomfort

Infested: A situation where many insects or animals would cause damage or disease

Ingest: To swallow; to absorb

Injured: Hurt; harmed; damaged; impaired

Instantaneously: Immediately; something that happens right away; all of the sudden

Intact: In one piece; complete; not damaged

Intelligible: A message that can be understood; something that is said or written clearly

Intrigued: Curious; fascinated

Item: A thing; an object

Join: To get together; to connect. **Rejoin:** To get together, to connect again

Literally: Exactly what is said, word for word

Mock: To tease; to make fun of something or someone

Network: A group of people or things that are connected to each other

Nightmares: Bad dreams

Notice: To pay attention to something

Numerous: A lot, or many

Oblivious: Not being aware of something; not knowing what is happening

Odor: (bad) Smell

Orbit: A curved path on an object (like a satellite) around a planet

Parasite: An organism that lives inside or on another organism

Perennial: Something that lasts forever; something that is always the same way

Pervasive: Spread everywhere

Pleasant: Nice; something that gives a feeling of happiness

Precious: Adorable; valuable

Precise: Exact; very accurate

Predict: To know what will happen in the future

Proceed: To start or continue an activity; to go as planned

Properly: Correctly; appropriately

Recall: To remember

Refrain: To hold back; to stop from doing something

Remote: Far

Repel: to push something away. **Repellent:** something that pushes away, that makes you sick, disgusted or uncomfortable

Reveal: to tell others something that is surprising, new

Retrieve: To get back something

Rural: Countryside; not in a big city

Rush hour: A time of the day where there is heavy traffic

Saga: A long story, full of events

Sarcasm: (1) Using words that mean the opposite of what you want to say or (2) making fun of someone or something

Satellite: An object that circles around a planet

Satisfaction: Enjoyment of accomplishing a goal

Section: A part of something; a piece of something bigger

Settling: Calming; relaxing

Shiver: To shake; to tremble

Shriek: A high-pitched scream

Slime: A wet, slippery, and usually disgusting substance

Smirk: A smile meaning that someone knows a secret or that someone feels victorious

Solitary: Alone, not being surrounded by other people

Soothing: Calming; something that reduces pain or discomfort

Sparse: Few and far from each other; scattered

Spectacular: Something that is very beautiful, that is impressive

Stalagmite: A type of icicle that is raising from the floor of the cave, and it is formed by minerals and water

Stalactite: A type of icicle that is typically hanging from the ceiling of a cave, and it is formed by minerals and water

Station: A place where certain activities happen

Stoic: A person that endures negative feelings (like shame or pain) without showing his or her feelings

Succeed: To reach a goal; to have success at what you planned to do

Suffocate: To have difficulty breathing or to die because of the lack of air to breathe

Suggest: To advise; to propose something

Suitable: Appropriate; well fit; just right

Suspicion: A feeling that something is possible, or true

Swift: Quick; speedy

Terrifying: Very scary; horrific

Triple: Three times as much

Typical: Usual; classic; something that is specific to a thing or a person

Urge: (1) A strong need or (2) To push or to convince somebody to do something

Vigorous: Strong and full of energy

ABOUT THE AUTHOR

Dacian Dolean, PhD is an educational psychologist and a reading research scientist specialized in language and literacy development of elementary and middle school students. His goal is to help bridging the existing gap between academic research and classroom practice. While he has authored and co-authored several scientific papers and he has developed multiple curriculum instructional and testing materials for classroom teachers, this is his first novel. The novel was written with the purpose of improving vocabulary and reading comprehension of middle grade readers (ages 8 through 12) by introducing them intentionally and systematically to Tier 2 and Tier 3 (academic) vocabulary. For more information, go to www.drdolean.com, or follow him on Twitter @DDolean

Made in the USA
Las Vegas, NV
23 November 2022

60031449R00098